Praise for Timothy Carter

Epoch

"In this fast-paced novel, readers will identify with Vincent's ability to see goodness in the world, and will root for him and his companions ... overall, *Epoch* is entertaining."
—School Library Journal

"This novel is sure to please most young adult readers and will have particular appeal for younger boys ... HIGHLY REC-OMMENDED."
—CM: Canadian Review of Materials

Evil?

"A book that doesn't take itself too seriously, but will leave readers with plenty to consider, as it addresses themes of morality, sexuality, and faith."
—Publishers Weekly

"This laugh-filled romp will supply the right reader with a thing or two to think about ... educational as well as vastly entertaining."
—Kirkus Reviews

"Satirical, downright funny, and also thought-provoking, whether read as a somewhat titillating and action-filled fantasy or as a deeper treatise on the origins and meaning of evil."
—CM: Canadian Review of Materials

D1468807

"Quite a funny book. Carter has caught the voice of the quirky character that is Stuart, and the pace of the story is masterful."
—Resource Links Magazine

"Stuart's lightly delivered narrative and the fast-paced, tense story make *Evil?*, hands down (pun intended), an enthralling read."
—CharlottesLibrary.blogspot.com

the Cupid WAR

For my sister Claire, who helps me navigate the dark.

timothy carter

the Cupid WAR

All Love Is Warfare

flux™
Woodbury, Minnesota

First Edition
First Printing, 2011

Book design by Steffani Sawyer
Cover design by Ellen Dawson
Heart image on cover and part pages © iStockphoto.com/Adrian Niederhäuser

Flux, an imprint of Llewellyn Worldwide Ltd.

Library of Congress Cataloging-in-Publication Data
Carter, Timothy, 1972–
   The Cupid war / Timothy Carter.—1st ed.
      p. cm.
   Summary: Seventeen-year-old Ricky Fallon was contemplating suicide when he slipped and fell, only to find himself a Cupid in the afterlife, but between the bad boss, a pink bodysuit, and attacks from shadowy entities called Suicides, he is not feeling much love.
   ISBN 978-0-7387-2614-4
   [1. Future life—Fiction. 2. Love—Fiction. 3. Spirits—Fiction.
4. Suicide—Fiction. 5. Humorous stories.] I. Title.
   PZ7.C24825Cup 2011
   [Fic]—dc22

                                                    2011010480

Flux
Llewellyn Worldwide Ltd.
2143 Wooddale Drive
Woodbury, MN 55125-2989
www.fluxnow.com

Printed in the United States of America

Acknowledgments

There are always many people in need of thanking for bringing a book to life. Here are the biggies. I'd like to start off by thanking my wife, Violet, for her support, encouragement, and love. Next, I'd like to thank Acquisitions Editor Brian Farrey, for seeing this book's potential; Robert Brown, for being an excellent agent; Sandy Sullivan, for her fantastic editing; and Indigo Spirit manager Lori Mac-Dougall, for having me in to do so many signings.

I would also like to thank the Mood Disorders Association of Ontario (MDAO) for their wonderful staff, programs, group meetings, and facilitators (like Catherine, Barb, James & Fey, to name a few). They continue to help many people coping with a mood disorder, myself among them.

And finally, in no particular order, my thanks to the organizers and volunteers of Polaris, Ad Astra, Anime North, Con-Cept, and other fantastic SF/Fantasy conventions; Tim Hortons, for their life-giving steeped tea; Stephen Moffat, Matt Smith et al, for another terrific series of Doctor Who; and the Source, for the never-ending flow of fun ideas.

prologue

Ricky Fallon sat on the bridge railing, preparing to jump. It seemed like the least painful way to die, while ensuring the best chance for success.

He also wanted to cause the least amount of trouble for the city; his father believed a jumper was involved every time there was a delay on the subway. Fallon didn't want his dad to think he was inconsiderate. At least, no more than he already did.

That left bridges, and the only ones high enough were the two that spanned the Don Valley. The bridge of choice for most jumpers had been the Prince Edward Viaduct, but city planners had finally made good on their promise to build a safety fence along both sides. It was an eyesore for people driving by on the parkway below, but as a suicide stopper, it was most effective.

The Pape Street Bridge, however, had no such fence. Fallon had left his house at midnight, taken a bus to the bridge, and prepared himself for the final solution to his troubled life. For Fallon, there wasn't one specific reason for wanting to die. At least, he reflected, it wasn't *entirely* one specific reason.

Yes, he was upset over losing Becky. He took out his cell phone and looked at the only decent picture he had of her, the one he'd taken on their third date. That had been a good day. One of my last, Fallon thought, as he set the phone aside on the ledge.

Yes, he hated getting yelled at by his father because he was too sloppy, he wasn't doing well enough at school, he didn't show enough initiative, he wasn't like his big sister, or he'd turn out just like his mother.

Yes, he hated his mother. She'd named him Ricky shortly before she'd run out on him and his father and sister. And then she had to go and get killed by a drunk driver before she could apologize and make things right.

All that had made him hate his life, but Susan had driven him to the point of death.

Susan Sides was his closest, dearest, bestest friend. At least, she liked to think so. Their French teacher had paired them for a *dictée* over a year ago, and Susan took that to mean they should be friends forever.

And Susan needed a friend. Her family hated her,

boys thought she was ugly, and none of the girls would hang out with her. That was what she'd told Fallon, every single day, for the last year. And during that year, Fallon's own life had fallen down the crapper.

Boy, did it ever, Fallon thought. Even now, as he stood ready to end it all, he couldn't believe things had gone as badly as they had.

It had started in small ways. He'd found it hard to get to sleep, and even harder to get out of bed. His appetite went down, and so did his grades. He stopped finding joy in things, and every endeavor seemed a huge effort. Problems with his father began in earnest, and the school bullies came out of the woodwork to hammer him with everything they had. Fallon felt like he had a heavy wet blanket wrapped around his heart, and it grew heavier whenever Susan was near.

He'd tried to get her to make other friends. No one else wanted to befriend her, and Susan herself didn't want to try.

"I don't need a whole bunch of friends," she'd told him. "I just need one friend. You!"

He'd tried to get her some counseling. Susan refused to get any kind of help. Why would she need professional help, she said, when all she really needed was one good friend to listen? It never occurred to him that he might need counseling himself; all his efforts had been for her.

Fallon had tried reasoning with her. He'd asked her to only unload her problems on him if it was an emergency.

"But when I have a problem," she'd replied, "it is an emergency!"

He'd said he needed more free time.

"But the time you spend with your friends is your free time!"

"I need to spend more time with Becky," he'd tried. "She's my girlfriend, after all."

"But you're my only friend!" Susan had said. "If I didn't get to spend time with you, I'd…"

She hadn't needed to finish. Fallon knew what she would say.

"If I didn't have you," she'd told him once, "I'd kill myself."

Of course Becky had dumped him. He was spending all his time with another girl. Besides, he'd changed since they'd started seeing each other. Now he was moody and tired all the time, and no fun at all. She had, however, given him one chance.

"Drop the loser," she'd said, "or we're done."

Fallon hadn't wanted to break up with Becky, but he didn't want Susan to kill herself, either. He knew she would; after all, she told him she'd tried before.

He had to choose between his relationship and her life.

"Don't you run out on your friend," his father told him. "That's what your mother would do."

"I'm not like Mom," he'd said.

"Prove it," his father replied.

Fallon proved it, Becky broke up with him, and Susan clung to him for another three months. She would cling to him forever if he gave her the chance. Fallon didn't want to give her that chance. He wanted out. He wanted freedom.

However, as he sat on the edge looking down at the barely visible Don River below, Fallon changed his mind. It wasn't because of a ray of light from Heaven, or an angel appearing to tell him there was a better way. Instead, Fallon changed his mind due to a very simple realization. On Monday morning at school, there would be shock. By the afternoon, however, there would be jokes. He called himself Fallon. The word "fall" was right there in the name. Sure, it was pronounced differently, but he knew his classmates would make the connection.

"A guy named Fallon falls to his death. What're the odds of that?"

"Fall-on really lived up to his name, huh?"

"I guess swallowing a bottle of pills just wouldn't have been appropriate."

In the latter part of his life, he'd been a joke. Did he really want to be a joke in death? Sure, he'd get a page of the yearbook all to himself, but did he really want to be remembered as a punch line?

And so, with a heavy heart and a loud sigh, he swung his legs back onto the ledge. He had no idea how he would get through the next day or the next week—he didn't even know how he was going to get home—but he'd manage somehow, he supposed.

Fallon stood up to hop down from the concrete railing. As he did so, he slipped on the cell phone he'd left there, and fell backward off the bridge.

pART 1

1

Fallon hovered over his body, dead. His body lay on the grassy floor of the Don Valley, crumpled and still. There was a small puddle of rainwater less than a meter from his right side; in it, Fallon could see a softball-sized sphere of light. Instinctively, he knew the ball of light was his soul.

Fallon couldn't quite believe what had just happened. He'd set out with suicide on his mind, true enough, but he'd changed his mind in the end, hadn't he? Yes, he remembered doing it, but that didn't make him any less dead.

So, he wondered, what was he now? What would come next? Was he supposed to feel at peace? Sad? Guilty for all the wrong things he'd done? Happy that it was all over?

First and foremost, he felt better. The weight he'd been carrying around in his heart was gone. Of course, so was his heart. Nevertheless, he felt better than he had in ages, and it was quite a rush. He could turn his life around, make things right. He'd make his father proud, and maybe even win Becky back.

Except, he was dead. He'd had his chance.

It occurred to him that when news of his death reached Susan, she might kill herself to join him. That thought filled him with more terror than anything he'd felt before. He also realized he might end up meeting his mother. He wasn't ready for that, not yet. If it did happen, however, he'd have a few choice words to say to her.

Fallon became aware of a presence. He'd read about people who'd had near-death experiences seeing deceased loved ones on the Other Side, and he feared his mother had come after all. Don't be my mom, he thought.

He didn't turn to face the presence; he didn't have a body any more, so the old rules didn't apply. Instead, Fallon willed his light-ball form to change its perception. To his relief, he saw it wasn't his mother—it was a bald man, standing next to some bushes a couple of meters away.

The man appeared both naked and clothed; he looked naked, but there did appear to be a thin, skin-tight stocking on his pale form. An aura of brightness flowed out gently from his body, so Fallon guessed he was an angel.

Fallon expected him to offer words of comfort, then invite him to embark on a wondrous journey into the Light. He was surprised, then, when the angelic being said:

"Another goddamn jumper. Just great."

Okay, Fallon thought. Not the reception I was hoping for.

"Let's go, buddy," said the glowing man. He raised his right hand, and Fallon found himself floating toward him. When he arrived in front of his angelic companion, the world as he knew it vanished. The bushes, the puddle, his body, the bridge, the entire Don Valley simply faded away into nothingness.

"What the … ?" Fallon said, his voice sounding like a bad recording of its former self. He didn't say the words so much as project them from his mind. At least I can still talk, he thought.

"Where am I?" he asked, looking around. He felt like he was in a room, even though he could see no walls. He didn't think it was Heaven, because it wasn't bright enough. He also didn't think it was Hell, because it wasn't all that dark. He was in a literal gray area.

"What is this place?" he asked, his first question having garnered no response.

"Shut it," the angelic being said.

"You know," Fallon said, "for an angel, you're mighty surly."

"I'm not an angel," the being said. "I'm Bud. And I told you to shut it. I'm trying to assess you."

"Assess me?" Fallon said.

Bud held his hands on either side of Fallon's soul and concentrated.

"You were gonna off yourself," Bud said. "We don't look kindly on that."

"But I didn't kill myself," Fallon said. "It was an accident."

"I know," Bud said. "But you were planning it. Life is the gift, and there's nothing we hate more than souls who throw away that gift."

"Um, who's we?" Fallon asked.

"Soul Reapers," Bud said, "like me. We collect souls and send them where they belong."

"And where do I belong?"

"If you'll stop bugging me," Bud said, "I'll figure that out."

"Right, sorry," Fallon said, and he kept quiet while Bud did his thing.

"Pretty ordinary teenager, weren't ya?" Bud said, dropping his hands back to his sides. "Think the whole world spins for you, and not a thought about making it better. Typical."

"Get bent, baldy," Fallon said.

Bud glared at him. "What was that?"

"Oh, did I hurt your feelings, chromedome?" Fallon asked.

"You'd better take that back," Bud said.

"Why should I?" Fallon said. "I'm dead, this is the

afterlife, and I don't know what's going on. Instead of filling me in, you've been treating me like crap. Well, it stops now."

Bud stared at him silently for a few moments, giving Fallon time to consider what he was doing. Basically, he was telling off the one being who currently had control of his fate. Not the smartest thing to do.

"Okay, kid," Bud said, his features softening. "I was in your position once. And you're not the jumper I thought you were. Maybe I should take the time to fill you in. Only fair. Basically, your karma's really high."

"My karma?" Fallon said.

"Every soul has karma," Bud told him. "It's the stuff your soul has to work through, the things you do to become a better person. Some people work off their karma by the time they die, and there's a place for them that you'd think of as Heaven. Then there's the rest, the people like you, who didn't use their lives the way they should. If you didn't work it off in your life, you have to work it off now."

"Nobody told me that was the deal!" Fallon said. "If I'd known that…"

"But that's the point, isn't it?" Bud said. "The people who work it off naturally don't need to be told. It's about choosing to do better, something you didn't give a lot of thought to."

"Okay," Fallon said. "So what happens now?"

"Now," Bud said, "I'm taking you to the guy who knows how to deal with your type."

"Oh yeah?" Fallon said.

"Yeah," Bud replied. "His name's Louis, and he's gonna wipe that attitude clean out of ya. You, pretty boy, are gonna be a Cupid."

2

A Cupid?" Fallon asked. "You mean ... ?"
"That's right," Bud replied. "You're going to make people fall in love."

"Oh," Fallon said. When it came to afterlife assignments, this wasn't what he'd been expecting.

"My man Louis runs the Cupids," Bud said. "He'll teach you a thing or two."

"Can't wait," Fallon said.

"And quit with the lip," Bud said.

"Sorry, sir," Fallon said, glaring at Bud's back. He was not having a good night, and this bozo wasn't making things any easier. Was this really the afterlife, or was he just having a bad dream? Wasn't death supposed to be a wondrous journey to a better place? There'd been a lot of books about that.

Of course, there had been a lot of books that suggested another possibility. Books, and pamphlets, and of course tracts. He remembered getting one such tract from the religious club at school. In it, a faceless God judged a man, found him guilty, and threw him into a pit filled with flames.

So, all things considered, Fallon's afterlife could have been a lot worse.

The grayness around them changed, and Fallon found himself in another room. This one was pink, and there were heart shapes decorating the walls.

"Cute," Fallon said. "But way cliché."

"Wait here," Bud said. "I'll get Louis."

Bud walked toward one of the walls and passed through it. Fallon wondered if he could do the same thing, but when he tried, the room moved with him. He projected himself at each of the walls, then tried the floor and ceiling. Every time, the room moved with him. Escape, it seemed, was not a possibility.

Fallon waited. There was nothing else to do. The hearts stared back at him from the walls, mocking him.

"Tryin' to bail already?"

Fallon shifted his perspective to the speaker, who'd arrived behind him. Like Bud, he wore a skin-tight stocking, but his was a darker pink and had a red heart as a chest emblem. He looked older than Bud, more weatherbeaten, like a man who's seen it all and probably doesn't approve. His hair was dark and military-short, and his eyes were a sharp green.

Bud appeared through the wall behind him. "Guess he moved around a bit," he said. "Louis, meet Richard Fallon. Richard, meet Louis Baker."

"Call me Fallon," Fallon said.

"I'll call you whatever I like," Louis replied. "You call me Mr. Baker or sir, got that? Now, let's get you prepped and ready to work with a new body."

"New body?" Fallon asked.

"Well, you're not thinkin' of goin' around like that, are ya?" Louis asked with a hint of a snicker. "You need one of these"—he poked himself—"if you're going to be of any use to me."

"But I thought…" Fallon stopped. What was the point? He clearly didn't know the rules here. "Okay, fine. Give me a body."

"Ever heard of the word 'please'?" Louis said. "Dead teenagers, I tell ya. No respect."

"Okay," Fallon said. "Mr. Baker, sir, may I please, pretty please, have a body so I can do the job you want me to do?"

"What have I told you about lip?" Bud said.

Louis turned to the Soul Reaper. "Bud, why don't you go get the protomatter while I tell the newbie here how we do things?"

"You got it," Bud replied, and he smiled an evil smile at Fallon before vanishing into the wall.

"You think you're something special, don't you?" Louis returned his attention to Fallon. "Yeah, I get your type all the time."

If Fallon had eyes, he would have rolled them. If this was the man responsible for the world's love, little wonder there were so many divorces.

"Let me guess," he said. "You're gonna show me that I'm nothing. I'm going to learn what hard work really is, and you're gonna be my teacher. I've heard it all."

"Not yet, you haven't," Louis replied. "You're in my world now, boy, and my world's no place for slackers who aren't willing to put in a day's work. You think the universe revolves around you?"

As Louis bore into him with a well-practiced lecture about hard work and making something of himself, Fallon tried to tune him out. He couldn't, however; Louis's words reminded him of his father's lectures, especially the one he'd received after quitting his first and only job.

Back in eleventh grade, Fallon had landed a position in the produce department of a new grocery superstore. Six weeks later, he'd quit in disgust. The store managers had completely unrealistic work expectations, and they'd treated all the new hires with contempt. Fallon's supervisor, a fat little troll named Carmella Lanniki, had been particularly abusive, offering vague directions and then ranting when things weren't done properly. Fallon had left in the middle of one such rant, waving his middle finger behind his back.

His father had not been amused. And when Fallon told him about the abusive conditions at the store, he did not find a sympathetic ear.

"You can't go through life giving up every time things get hard," his father had said. "Do you think the world revolves around you? Should everything come to a stop just because you're not happy with the way you're being treated? That won't happen, son."

"But Dad..."

"Your mother left us when things got tough," his father had said. "If you don't want to turn out like her, you'd better get your act together."

As Louis chewed him out, Fallon couldn't help but think that his dad (and, quite possibly, Carmella) was having the last laugh.

"Are you done?" he cut in, knowing full well that Louis was not. "I really don't need you to tell me how important you think you are. And as for respect? You want it, earn it. I've had my fill of jerks, thank you very much."

Louis's upper lip curled into a sneer, but Fallon was completely unafraid. Sure, he was in Louis's world, but what could the guy really do to him? Fallon was dead, and not getting any deader.

"You watch your mouth," Louis said. "Just because you're dead doesn't mean you can't get hurt."

Before Fallon could wonder if Louis had read his thoughts, Bud came back with a solid cube of pink matter.

"Your new body," Bud said, tossing the cube at Fallon.

As soon as the cube made contact, it flowed all around Fallon's soul like hot liquid metal. He fell to the floor as gravity suddenly reintroduced itself, and he felt himself forming. Arms and legs sprouted out of him, followed by his new head. In moments it was over; his new body was fully grown.

Fallon pulled his new self together and stood up. He felt different—lighter, for one thing. He didn't feel as free as he had when he'd been a soul, but it was lots better than his previous existence.

He felt his face, and wondered if it looked the same as when he'd been alive. There were no mirrors around, so there was no way to tell.

"How do I look?" he asked his silent audience.

"Like a dweeb," Bud said. "But don't take it too hard. All Cupids look like dweebs."

"Hey," said Louis, giving Bud a good-natured punch on the arm.

"Come on, your guys wear pink and have red hearts on your chests," Bud said. "What other word is there?"

At that, Fallon looked down. He was indeed clad in a pink suit with a red heart on his chest. It was skin-tight, leaving nothing to the imagination. He had an aver-age build, with arms and legs slightly bigger and more muscled than when he'd been alive. Something, however, seemed to be missing...

"Hey!" Fallon cried. "I have no...where's my..."

Louis and Bud burst out laughing. Fallon felt between his legs to see if he'd missed it, but there was nothing. The sight of him searching made his audience laugh even harder.

"I was wondering when he was gonna notice," Bud said as he turned and walked through the wall behind him. "He's all yours, Louis."

3

"Come on, joke's over," Fallon said with barely con-cealed anger. "You've had your fun, now stop being a jerk and give me my missing... parts."

Louis sniggered a moment longer. Then his face grew serious.

"Never call me a jerk," Louis said, and he raised his arms and pointed his fingers at Fallon. Electric bolts fired from his fingertips and hit Fallon in his brand-new shoulder. Fallon jumped in surprise and mild pain, like he'd just received a static electricity shock.

"Just a little taste of what you'll get if you give me any more attitude," Louis said, pointing his thumb and index finger like a gun. "You want another demonstration?"

Before Fallon could answer, Louis fired off another

bolt. This one hit Fallon right between the eyes and knocked him back a few inches.

"Hey!" Fallon said. "Quit it!"

"Gotta have discipline," Louis said. "Otherwise there'd be too many like you messing with me. You gonna be good?" Fallon nodded stiffly, and Louis lowered his hand.

"If you could have shocked me all this time," Fallon asked, "why didn't you … "

"Not until you had a body," Louis said. "Come with me and I'll fill you in on what you need to know."

Louis walked into one of the pink walls and disappeared. Fallon, half expecting the room to follow him again, took a tentative step forward. The wall got closer; it seemed he was well and truly one of them now. He walked confidently forward into the wall and smacked himself against it.

"Ow," he said.

"Forgot to tell ya." Louis stuck his head back through. "Ya haveta think your way through walls like these."

"Okay," Fallon said. "How do I do that?"

"With your mind, dum-dum."

"Do all newly dead people have to go through this?" he asked.

"Nope," Louis replied. "Just the ones with attitude. Now smarten up and come with me." Louis stepped backward and his head vanished again.

"If this isn't Hell," Fallon muttered, "please send me there. It's gotta be better than this."

He tried thinking his way through, and stepped through the wall with no trouble. Then he did a double take; the next room wasn't a room at all, but a palace. He stood beneath a huge pink dome that stretched from the wall behind him off into a near-infinite distance. A big red heart was superimposed on the dome's ceiling, and the area beneath it bustled with activity. There were rows upon rows of big red cubes. People in pink outfits were walking around and in between those cubes, on a floor of solid white.

"This is the Cupid Center, our main headquarters," Louis said, walking over to the nearest red cube. "I keep track of all the Cupids, where they're placed, what they're doing. All that stuff. You see this?" He patted the cube next to him. It was the size of a refrigerator, taller than any of the others. "This is what Love looks like. Pure, uncorrupted Love."

"That's ... love?" Fallon said, approaching slowly. On closer inspection, the cube looked like a big block of fudge.

"That's what I said," Louis told him. Then, to Fallon's surprise and horror, he broke off a chunk and started snacking.

"What," Fallon asked, "are you doing?"

"Recharging," Louis replied, taking another bite.

"Uh huh," Fallon said. "Are you going to start making sense anytime soon?" He braced himself for another electric shock, and he was not disappointed. He gritted his teeth and managed to keep from crying out, but just barely.

"That ain't your old body, kiddo," Louis said. "Can't go for cheeseburgers like you used to. Your new body's a Cupid body, and the only thing you can eat is this." Louis ripped another chunk of Love off the cube and tossed it to Fallon. "Eat that. All first timers get one bite for free to get them started. The rest, you gotta earn."

Fallon looked at the brick of Love in his hands and thought about all that had been said and written about love throughout the ages. All the sonnets, poems, and greeting cards, and all the boy-band songs. Love, he'd heard, was the answer. God is love, the spiritualists said. Love made the world go 'round, love is the most powerful force in the universe.

Fallon wondered if all those things would have been said if the speakers knew that love was a bunch of big chunks of red fudge.

He took a bite. The Love had a syrupy texture, and tasted like corn and cheese. That figures, he thought.

"Like it?" Louis asked. "Well, better get used to it. That's all you get to eat, forever."

Fallon popped the rest into his mouth. *I'll get bored of this real quick*, he thought. "So, how do I get my own Love?"

"Ya gotta earn it, like I said," Louis told him. "Learn to listen. Now come with me."

Louis walked off at a brisk clip, and Fallon followed

him. They walked for ages down the rows of Love, not stopping or even slowing down. Fallon thought he'd be tired, but that didn't seem to be a problem for his new body.

They walked the entire way in silence. Fallon had a lot of questions, such as where did the Love come from, but he didn't particularly want to talk to Louis. If there was something he needed to know to do his job, Louis would tell him in his own time.

Finally, they arrived at the far end of the domed enclosure. There were several rounded arches built into the wall; to Fallon, they resembled doorways, but the space inside the arches looked as solid as the rest of the wall.

"Gonna ask me what these are?" Louis asked, indicating the arches with a flick of his head.

"Okay," Fallon said, making an effort not to roll his eyes. "What are they?"

"Portals," Louis said. "They transport you from here to the place where you're gonna work."

"Gotcha," Fallon said. "Walk through one and you're somewhere else, like a teleporter."

"Teleporter?" Louis said. "What are you, a geek? They're portals, like I said. Gonna ask me how they work?"

"How do they work?" Fallon asked, gritting his teeth. He was getting mighty sick of this guy.

"You stand at a portal and think of where you wanna go," Louis told him as he walked to the nearest one. "The portal takes that information and makes a doorway to the place." As he spoke, the pink part of the wall enclosed by the portal's arch shimmered and took on a blue hue. "Blue means you're ready to go. The doorway stays open until another Cupid thinks up some other place."

"So if I wanted to go to New York," Fallon said, "it would … "

"You're not going to New York," Louis said. "You're here to work, remember? Follow me and we'll get you started."

Louis stepped into the portal and vanished into the blue. Fallon made a rude gesture behind his back, then followed.

4

They appeared back in the world, inside a large grocery store. Fallon recognized it immediately; it was
the store where he used to work.

"Can this day get any worse?" he said. "Louis, why are
we here?"

"This was part of your life," Louis replied. "We always
train new Cupids in a place that's familiar. Makes it easier."

"Won't people see us?" Fallon asked, wrapping his
arms over the heart on his chest. The last thing he wanted
was to be seen by someone he knew in this outfit.

"Didn't I tell ya?" Louis said. "We exist on a different
level than this world does. Something to do with vibration.

I don't wanna get into it. Basically, it means we're invisible and can't touch nothing. Come on, let's go find Caleb."

They set off through the store. Louis walked through display stands, shopping carts, and even people as if they weren't there. Fallon found himself walking around the things and people in his way. Old habits from life were hard to break.

However, the people he was avoiding did not seem to notice him at all. Plus, when he backed out of the way of a shopping cart, he found himself in the middle of another. The man pushing that cart walked straight through him, leaving Fallon weirded out but unharmed. There was no sensation at all.

"O-kay," he said. "That was interesting."

He wanted to experiment with his new-found insubstantialness, but knew he'd get another shock if he didn't keep up with Louis. He turned in the direction his new boss had been walking, but Louis was nowhere to be seen.

Fallon let off a most uncupidlike curse, then hurried off in search. There was an aisle of fresh vegetables ahead, which Fallon had stocked once upon a life. Louis might have walked through that, so he hurried to do the same.

He emerged on the other side of the aisle, passing through jumbo packs of napkins and toilet paper. He looked around for Louis, but still couldn't see him.

What he could see stopped him dead in his tracks. Becky, his ex-girlfriend, was walking toward him, idly pushing a cart. Her mother walked along behind, scanning the aisles for items.

Fallon realized it was probably only the morning after his death here in the living world. His body might not have been identified yet, so Becky didn't know he was dead.

"Beck…" he said, not moving as her cart started to pass through him. He reached out a hand to touch her hair, but he could not. Becky and her mother walked through him, never noticing he was there.

Fallon turned, watching them go. He wondered how she would feel when she finally did learn of his untimely passing. They'd had a pretty good thing going before Susan arrived and ruined everything. If only he'd told Susan to buzz off when he'd first met her. If only he'd tried harder to make things work out. Fallon watched Becky and her mother turn the corner and vanish from view, and wished for what could never be.

Then an electric jolt struck him, and he fell to his knees.

"You got hearing problems, mister?" Louis said as he stormed over to him. "I told you to come with me, and as soon as I turn my back, you go off cruisin' for chicks."

"I lost you," Fallon said as he stood back up.

"Learn to keep up," Louis said, giving him another shock. "You're not here to goof off, you're…"

"…here to work, I know," Fallon said.

"You better," Louis said. "Now let's go find Caleb."

"Right here, Louis."

Fallon and Louis turned to see a large man in a pink Cupid uniform casually walking toward them. He was tall, dark-skinned, and bearded, with a serious face but a fun, knowing spark in his eyes.

"Still tormenting the newcomers, I see," Caleb went on as he approached. "I'm amazed you have any life force left."

"I have enough for you, Caleb," Louis warned. "So watch it."

Caleb seemed to regard the threat with amusement. He turned his attention to Fallon and extended a large hand.

"Welcome to the Cupids," he said. "I'm Caleb Williams."

"I'm Fallon."

"His name's Richard Fallon," Louis said.

"Do you prefer Richard or Fallon?" Caleb asked.

"Fallon," he replied. "I hate Richard. And especially Ricky."

"Nobody cares," Louis said. "And you'll call him Mr. Williams."

"Call me Caleb," Caleb said, a hint of a smile on his lips. "That is what I prefer."

"You're asking for it," Louis said, raising his hand.

"Very well then." Caleb turned toward him. "Get it out of your system." He spread his arms and waited.

Fallon stared at him, wide-eyed. What did he think he was doing?

Louis hesitated, looked from Fallon to Caleb, then lowered his arm. "Just don't forget who the boss is," he said, a tad nonplussed.

"Consider me adequately corrected," Caleb said, looking amused once more.

"Well, you show Ricky here what he has to do," Louis said. "I'll check back later."

With that, Louis turned, walked through the aisle of bathroom tissue, and vanished from view.

"I am sorry for what you have had to suffer," Caleb said. "Louis is not the easiest person to get along with. A piece of work, you might say."

"I'd say he's a piece of something else," Fallon said, and Caleb chuckled.

"Sometimes he is," he agreed. "But he has his reasons. Especially in a place like this."

"What, a grocery store?"

"Yes," Caleb said. "He was the deli manager for a store outside of Washington for thirty-four years. He died and joined the Cupids after a former employee shot him."

"Yikes," Fallon said. *Can't say I blame the guy that shot him,* he thought to himself.

"I'm sure it's nothing personal," Caleb said. "Try not to let him get to you. After all, forces greater than us have given him authority."

"Yeah, about that," Fallon said. "Why would those greater forces want a guy like him running Heaven?"

"This isn't Heaven," Caleb said. "We haven't earned that yet. If you are a Cupid, then you have something from your life to atone for."

"The karma thing," Fallon said. "Bud told me about that."

"Indeed," Caleb said. "There is good news, though. When you have paid your karma debt, you will move on."

"How long does that usually take?" Fallon asked.

"That depends," Caleb said, "on the level of your debt. I will teach you all about this life between life, Fallon, and I will answer what questions I can. Right now, though, I must begin your first Cupid lesson. It is not beyond Louis to hide and spy on new Cupids. We must at least pretend to be working."

"Gotcha," Fallon said, looking around. If Louis was spying, he could be anywhere, inside anything. He didn't need to hide behind a corner, not when he could walk through the wall.

Caleb started off down the nearest aisle and Fallon followed.

"You said something about Louis's life force," Fallon said as they walked.

"He uses up a bit of his spirit every time he shocks someone," Caleb replied. "I would bet my entire supply of Love that he has gone to rest and recharge himself."

"Is that why he didn't shock you?" Fallon asked, and Caleb smiled.

"No," he said. "Louis and I go back a ways. We know each other well. I don't think he really wants me as an enemy."

They turned into the cereal aisle. A short-haired brunette Fallon didn't recognize was stacking the shelves in front of them.

"This is Emily," Caleb told him. "She has feelings for one of the cashiers. I saw to that, shortly before you made your arrival. I'd like to see those feelings returned. Come with me."

Caleb led Fallon to the front of the store, where three cashiers were handling the lines of impatient customers. Caleb walked straight through the lines of people and stood behind the middle cashier, a teenage boy with long black hair tied back in a ponytail.

"I know him," Fallon said. "That's Mark Leder. We used to work together in produce. The manager always gave him grief about his hair."

"Were you friends?" Caleb asked, and Fallon nodded. "Good. Then a friend of yours is about to become a happy man."

Caleb stood behind Mark and slid his right hand into Mark's back. Mark didn't notice the intrusion into his person; all his attention was on the purchases of the customer beside the register.

"What I've done," Caleb said, "is put my hand into Mark's heart. Now we wait."

"For what?" Fallon asked.

"For his new love, of course," Caleb replied. "We left Emily over there." He indicated the aisle with a nod of his head. "Soon she will come into view, and she will look at young Mark here."

"How do you know she'll do that?" Fallon asked.

"Because she has feelings for him," Caleb said. "Look, there she is."

And she was. Emily turned the corner and cast a shy glance at Mark.

"Mark," Caleb said in the boy's ear, "look left."

To Fallon's surprise, Mark actually did turn to look in her direction. Then Fallon saw a small flash of pink light from Mark's chest.

Caleb removed his hand from Mark's torso and stood back to admire his handiwork. Mark smiled sheepishly back at the girl, waved awkwardly, then returned to his customers. A second later he looked up at her again.

"And that's what we do," Caleb said. "Any questions?"

"A few, yeah," Fallon replied. "Number one, what was the light show? And how come he could hear you? I thought we were on some kind of different vibrational level or something."

"We are," Caleb said, leading Fallon away. "Did you see my hand inside him? I was touching his heart, and his soul. When you touch another's soul, you can communicate with that soul, like a voice in the back of the mind. The person is likely not even aware of the communication, at least on a conscious level. Mark there"—Caleb nodded his head back in the cashier's direction—"will probably not even remember the voice. Or perhaps he will. That would be a very romantic thing to tell his love, that a voice from beyond told him to ... are you all right?"

They had walked out through the front entrance and were facing the half-filled parking lot. Fallon had stopped, his eyes wide with realization.

"When I first saw Becky, my ex-girlfriend," Fallon said, "I heard a voice in my head, too. I was in class, sitting at my desk reading a book, and a voice told me to look up. I did, and there was Becky. I ... fell in love with her right then."

"Ah, yes," Caleb said. "That would have been Cole's doing. I trained him, too."

"But that means I never really loved her!" Fallon said. He tried to lean against the side of the building, but instead he fell through it.

"That is not true," Caleb replied as he helped Fallon back up.

"Yes it is!" Fallon replied, shaking off Caleb's helping hand. "I just liked her because of what your buddy did to me. He ... that's what you guys do! You trick people into falling in love."

"No," Caleb replied. "That's not it at all, Fallon. What we do is the very thing that keeps the world turning."

"Oh, come off it!" Fallon said. "Don't give me that greeting-card crap. I've seen what love really looks like, and it's nothing but chunks of red fudge."

"Fallon," Caleb said, his voice serious, "I will tolerate any number of things, but I will not listen to anyone belittling the wonder that is love."

"Fine," Fallon said. "Keep your love." And he turned and ran off across the parking lot.

"Fallon! Come back," Caleb called after him, but Fallon did not stop.

5

Fallon ran, not bothering to look where he was going. It hardly mattered; it wasn't like he was going to run into anything. He went through cars, trees, houses, and people, farther and farther away from the grocery store, Caleb, and everything.

Eventually he stopped running, not because he was tired but because hiding seemed like a better idea. It occurred to him that a nice, big, solid object would make a good hiding place. He could walk into one of the houses, stand inside a wall, and wait for Caleb and Louis to stop looking for him.

Fallon turned in the direction of the nearest house, and realized he'd come back to his old neighborhood. His own house was just up ahead, and there was a police car idling in the driveway. Two police officers stood on the doorstep, their hats in their hands.

The middle-aged man they were talking to was his father.

Fallon knew what was going on. He was witnessing the report of his own death. His family was only now finding out about his fall from Pape Bridge.

As Fallon watched, his stepmother joined his dad on the doorstep. A moment later his big sister joined them, too.

Fallon collapsed onto the ground. This was too much for him. This was what he'd imagined would happen after his death, but having to see it being played out was simply not fair. He was dead now; he shouldn't be seeing this!

Out of the corner of his eye, Fallon thought he saw something dark...

Despair flooded through him, soaked him like a monsoon, stuck to him like tar. It was similar to the way he'd felt during the last year of his life, but that wasn't this bad. No, nothing was as sickening as this. Fallon wanted nothing more than to return to the bridge and throw himself off, on purpose this time, but he couldn't muster up the energy to move. And the feeling of hopeless despair kept getting worse, so much worse...

"You! Get off him!"

Pink light bathed him, and he heard something scream. A black form, part humanoid and part shadow, detached itself from him and raced away. The utter despair he felt began to fade, and Fallon was able to put two and two together.

"That thing," he said. "It did that to me?"

"Yes," said Caleb, standing behind him. "It's a lucky thing I found you or he would have taken you."

"What … is it?" Fallon asked, watching as the dark form scampered away down the street.

"That," Caleb replied, "is a Suicide. They are our enemies, Fallon, as I'm sure you've realized by now."

"We have enemies?" Fallon turned around to look up at Caleb. He wanted to stand back up, but couldn't quite manage that yet. "Why … didn't you … tell me?"

"You ran away, remember?" Caleb replied. He reached down and took hold of Fallon's arms, easily hefting him back to his feet. "You would have been safe with me. From all of this."

It was clear by his tone that he meant more than just the attack. Fallon looked back at his family on the doorstep and nodded silently.

"Come on, let's go," Caleb said, leading Fallon away. "Best leave them be. Staying here will only bring you pain."

Fallon wanted to stay, wanted to do something for his family. He had no energy to resist, however, so he allowed Caleb to direct him.

"How did you find me?" he asked after a while.

"I have ways," Caleb said. "Besides, where else would you have gone? You were alone, you were upset; it was only natural you would have gone home." He held up his hand and a soft glow spread out from his fingertips. The glow grew into an oval doorway, and Caleb helped Fallon walk through it.

"Neat trick," Fallon said as they emerged back in the heart-domed enclosure of the Cupid Center. "Will I be able to do that soon?"

"When you learn how," Caleb replied. "Are you feeling any better?"

"A little, yeah," Fallon said. "Not so ... devastated."

"Time you ate some more Love," Caleb said. "Best cure there is for a psychic attack. It's not far to my Love block. You can eat all you want then."

"Great," Fallon said.

They set out through the maze of Love cubes. It was difficult going for Fallon; each step felt like a huge effort.

"Tell me about Suicides," he said, hoping the conversation would distract him.

"Suicides are beings similar to us, only they feed on negative emotions," Caleb said. "They take your despair and magnify it until even the smallest problem seems insurmountable, then they feed on the negativity that results. And because Cupids deal in positive emotions, our despair is that much more powerful. That is why we must always be on our guard, and always consume plenty of Love before returning to the field."

Fallon thought about what Caleb had told him. "Do they attack living people?" he asked.

"Yes," Caleb replied. "People with severe depressive disorders are the victims of Suicides. Strong people struggle to hang on, to fight back with drugs and therapy. Weak ones, however … "

"Jump?" Fallon said quietly.

"Yes," Caleb replied.

Fallon stopped walking. "Is that what happened to me?" he asked. "Is that why I wanted to kill myself?"

"Yes," Caleb said simply. "Try not to think about it."

"How can I not think about it?" Fallon snapped. "I'm dead because some evil spirit got me. That's not … "

He stopped. He'd been going to say *that's not fair*. Fallon knew what his father would have said to that: *Who ever said life is fair?*

"That is why Cupids exist, Fallon," Caleb said. "We give people something pure and special, something worth living for. And we fight off those spirits who strive to make life miserable. We are here to make life better, Fallon. Not fair, just better."

They walked in silence for a while. Fallon's mood did not get better, and he still felt weak. He hadn't felt at all tired when he'd walked all the way across the vast expanse of the Cupid Center before, but this time he found it exhausting. The dark feelings the Suicide had given him had faded a bit, but Fallon couldn't shake them off.

Not after what Caleb had told him.

"How are you doing?" Caleb asked.

"How do you think?" Fallon replied.

"Nearly there," Caleb told him. "Hold on."

"I can't make it."

"Yes, you can."

"No, I can't."

"Yes, you can."

"No, I can't," Fallon said, and he fell forward and collapsed in a heap.

"Okay, you can't," Caleb said, squatting down beside him. "Tell you what. I'll go ahead and bring some Love back to you. Just wait here, okay?"

Fallon managed a thumbs-up. Caleb hurried off, leaving him to rest.

6

Fallon lay on the white floor of the Cupid Center, waiting for Caleb to return. He didn't want to move; the Suicide attack had drained both his mood and his energy. He figured he'd be panting, but his new body didn't need to breathe.

He waited for a while, then grew impatient. What was taking Caleb so long? He dragged himself into a sitting position to look, but could not see Caleb anywhere among the aisles of Love cubes.

Speaking of which, there was a suitcase-sized cube of Love a meter or so to his right. Stuff Caleb, Fallon thought, and he crawled his way over. He sat himself up next to the cube, then scraped off a chunk no bigger than a Snickers bar.

"Hey! What d'you think you're doing?"

Fallon turned his head and saw a Cupid running toward him. The guy was big and brawny but not that old; Fallon guessed late teens, early twenties.

"Whoa, easy," Fallon said. "This is your Love?"

"Yeah, it is," the Cupid said, a look of indignation on his face. "You're not going to eat that, are ya?"

"I just need a bite," Fallon said, and he stuffed the Love piece into his mouth.

"Hey!" the guy said. "I worked my butt off for that."

"It's supposed to make me feel better."

"What?" the guy said. "That's my Love! Cupids aren't allowed to eat from each other's Love. Where's yours?"

"I don't think I have one yet," Fallon said.

"Well, you better get some fast," the guy said. "You owe me."

"Are you even interested in why I'm lying here?" Fallon asked. "How about some concern, some compassion? Do you even care why I wanted your Love?"

"No!" the Cupid said. "All I care about is … "

"Owen! Not taking a break, are ya?"

The Cupid spun around at the voice. Fallon groaned; not him, not now.

"And what're *you* doing, Ricky?" Louis said, glaring down at him. "Takin' a little nap? This hard work concept something new to ya?"

"Go away," Fallon groaned, fully expecting to be shocked. But the way he was feeling, he simply didn't care.

When the shock didn't come, he looked closer at his Cupid boss. Louis looked exhausted; all that shocking really did suck the life out of him.

"That attitude won't get you very far here, Ricky," Louis told him. "Well? One of you going to tell me what's going on? Owen, how about you?"

"I was just coming in to eat," Owen said, "when I saw this guy snacking on my Love."

"Were you trying to steal from Owen's Love?" Louis asked Fallon. "That's the biggest offense we have, you know."

"He was waiting for me," Caleb said, arriving with two fistfuls of Love.

"What d'you think you're doin' with that?" Louis said, pointing at Caleb's haul. "He's gotta earn his own, and he ain't gonna do it lyin' around on ... "

"Oh, stop it!" Caleb said, and he tossed the Love down into Fallon's lap and stormed over to Louis. "He was attacked by a Suicide. We could have lost him. You, of all people, should respect that."

Louis's eyes went wide. So did Owen's. Fallon looked from them to Caleb, wondering what would happen next.

"Okay, he can have some of your Love," Louis said. "But only enough to get him back on his feet. Then it's back to work for both of you." With that, Louis turned and walked off.

"Hey, sorry dude," Owen said, kneeling beside Fallon.

"I didn't know you'd been … I'm sorry. Take some more of mine. But just a little bit, okay?"

"He'll be fine with what I brought him," Caleb said. "Eat up, Fallon."

Fallon did. Voraciously. It was still cheesy and corny, but it was the best cheese and corn he'd ever tasted in his life. And death.

"Feeling better?" Caleb asked, watching him lick his fingers clean.

"Oh, yeah," Fallon replied. "I haven't felt this good since … since … "

"I understand," Caleb said, reaching out a hand to help him up. "Don't think about past times, Fallon. That's where you will find you are weakest. Focus on the present."

"That's what Louis told me when I started," Owen said. "He was my mentor, you know. He says … "

"Owen—that's your name, right?" Fallon asked.

"Yeah."

"Get lost, Owen," Fallon said.

"What?" Owen said, the indignant look returning. "You get lost! This is my spot."

"Come on, Fallon." Caleb put an arm around his shoulders and led him away. "Time we were getting back to work."

They began the long trek back to the portals. Fallon found it much easier going this time around—he was no longer tired. Realizing he'd been completely healed from his attack, Fallon felt almost cheerful.

"I wouldn't get on Owen's bad side if I were you," Caleb said as they walked.

"Why not?" Fallon asked. "The guy's a jerk. He wouldn't help me out when I was desperate."

"True," Caleb replied. "But he is one of Louis's favorites."

"Oh," Fallon said. "Oh crap."

"Owen isn't that bad," Caleb went on. "He projects a tough outer shell to hide his guilt."

"Guilt?"

"You must have noticed he is your age, or close to it," Caleb said. "He died when he was young. Crashed his car while drunk. Killed himself and his girlfriend Jada. It's been three years now, but he still blames himself for it."

"Well, it was his fault," Fallon said.

"What's done is done," Caleb said. "Since that time, he's become a fine Cupid. So has Jada, incidentally. She's one of my favorite students. They both have their own designated neighborhoods to look after. Someday you will too."

As they walked, Fallon remembered something Caleb had said earlier.

"What did you mean," he asked, "when you told Louis that he of all people should respect a Suicide attack? Was he attacked once?"

"Not exactly," Caleb said. "Most Cupids have been

attacked by Suicides, actually. Some get over it, others can't. But Louis's story is more complicated than that. And personal."

"Ooh, do tell!" Fallon said. If there was dirt to be dished on Louis, he wanted every bit of it.

Caleb was silent for a few moments.

"Another time," he said at last. "I will tell you, Fallon. I believe every Cupid has a right to know some of the details. But not just yet. I'd ... rather wait for another time."

Fallon nodded as if he understood, which of course he did not. He could tell, however, that Caleb wished the matter dropped. That was fine by him. He could wait. After all, it didn't seem like he was going anywhere.

Five minutes later they arrived at the portals. They chose one, stepped through, and went back to work.

7

"Love, as I was explaining to you before, is what keeps this world turning," Caleb said.

Fallon listened as he and Caleb walked through the food court at the local mall. He'd come to this mall many times before his untimely death. It had been one of Susan's favorite things, coming here and getting a mint tea and blabbing about all of her problems.

Fallon shook his head to clear it. Bad memories would not help him.

"We don't trick people into falling in love, Fallon," Caleb went on, leading him out of the rows of tables and into the mall proper. "That is impossible. If two people aren't interested, or at least open to the possibility of being interested, there is nothing we can do."

"But you make people fall in love," Fallon said. "I saw you."

"Because Mark was open to a love relationship with Emily in the first place," Caleb said. "All he needed was a little boost. We provide that boost, Fallon. We help make love happen."

"So if I were to pick just anyone," Fallon said, gesturing around him at the shoppers, "and made them look at someone they didn't want to be with, it wouldn't work?"

"Not necessarily," Caleb said. "The mind does not always know what the heart wants."

"But then how do you know?"

"You will know," Caleb told him, "when you touch their heart. That's where all the answers are. I know this is all very confusing," he added, seeing the look on Fallon's face. "It will become clear to you after you've gained some experience. And that is what we are here to get."

They arrived at a set of escalators. Fallon recognized where they were; the escalators led up to the mall's cinema.

"We're going to the movies?" he asked.

"Yes," Caleb replied.

"Cool." Fallon stepped onto the escalator.

A moment later he realized he wasn't moving. Looking down, Fallon saw the escalator steps rising up out of his feet like they weren't there.

"I think that now," Caleb said without hiding his amusement, "would be an excellent time to tell you about stairs."

"Yeah, why don't you?" Fallon said, walking through the escalator railing to stand beside him.

"We are out of sync with the energy vibrations of this world," Caleb told him. "You see that when you walk through things, as you did just now."

"Yeah, I know that already."

"However, we need to interact with this world on some level or we couldn't do our jobs," Caleb said. "Look down. Your feet are firmly planted on the floor when they should sink through. Do you know why that is?"

"No idea," Fallon said.

"You don't sink through the floor," Caleb said, "because you do not believe you will. That belief sends messages to your body that cause your feet to vibrate more harmoniously with the surface beneath you."

"So if I stop believing," Fallon said, "I'll fall into the Earth."

"Yes," Caleb said. "But I don't think you will. No one has, yet. Belief in the ground under one's feet is too strong. Stairs, however, are another matter. Escalators and elevators as well. Your mind perceives them differently. You know you use them to ascend or descend to another level."

"So how do you go up when you need to?" Fallon asked.

"Like this," Caleb said, and he walked behind a man who was stepping onto the escalator. Caleb inserted his hand into the man's back, and when the man rose with the rising steps Caleb was dragged along behind.

"It's easy!" Caleb said. "Just touch the heart."

Fallon walked up behind a young woman and touched her heart as she stepped onto the escalator. He ascended with her; it wasn't jarring at all, just a smooth ride.

Caleb was waiting for him at the top.

"Don't let go straight away," he cautioned as Fallon and his ride reached the upper level. "Your mind needs to readjust to the new ground beneath you. Take a few steps with this lovely young lady—that's it—and when you think you are ready..."

"How will I know?" Fallon asked. The idea of falling through the floor did not appeal to him.

"Your mind works fast," Caleb said. "Trust it. Let go."

Fallon did so, and did not immediately fall through the floor. He took a couple of steps, watching his feet carefully, but the floor remained safely solid.

"It's like the glass floor," he said.

"Pardon?"

"In the CN Tower," Fallon said. "They have a glass floor on the observation deck. People are afraid to walk out onto it because they can see all the way down to the ground, but the glass is just as solid as the concrete around it."

"In other words, it's all in your mind," Caleb said. "Good analogy, though. I must remember that for my next trainee. Anyway, keep practicing. Who knows, you may become as good as me someday. Now come, let's go to the movies."

They entered the cinema and walked right through the ticket collectors. Fallon headed for a theater showing an action movie he'd been dying to see, but Caleb held him back.

"For the purposes of training," Caleb said, "we will get the best results from a romantic comedy. Follow me."

They entered a theater showing a film that Fallon wouldn't have gone to even if he'd been paid. *The Truth About Poodles*—about a man who adopted a fluffy white dog in order to woo the woman of his dreams—was exactly the sort of tripe he avoided with a passion.

"We don't have to watch the whole thing, do we?" he asked as Caleb selected an aisle. He looked at some of the guys in the half-filled audience and chuckled; they looked bored out of their minds.

"No, but you do have to watch some of it," Caleb replied, "so you'll be ready for the right moment. I'm sure you are familiar with celebrity love?"

"You mean those idiots who fall for famous people who they've only seen in movies or photos?"

"Precisely," Caleb said. "When that happens, it is usually because a Cupid has been doing exactly what we are about to do now. Practicing."

Fallon looked from the bored male faces to the screen, and put two and two together.

"We're gonna make those poor saps fall for Jenny Lane?" he asked, watching as the celebrity in question "acted." "No way, Caleb. That's just wrong. That's . . . manipulating people."

"It is practice," Caleb pointed out, "and it is harmless. Remember, it will only work if one of these gentlemen is open to feelings for Miss Lane."

"But they're never going to have her," Fallon said.

"The feelings we give them today will fade," Caleb said. "Unless we give them another boost later on. Which we will not do. Unrequited love always fades if it is not nurtured, Fallon. Sometimes it becomes obsession, but such instances are rare. And doing this"—he reached into one of the guys' hearts just as Jenny got a close-up—"is the only practical way to practice without causing undue hurt."

The teen's chest glowed and suddenly he became interested in the movie. Very interested.

"Now you try," Caleb said.

"Okay," Fallon said, looking around. "Who should I start with?"

"Try anyone," Caleb said, "and see what their heart tells you."

Fallon shrugged and walked into the aisle, then picked a Japanese man sitting in mid-row. He walked around behind his seat and plunged his right hand into the guy's back. He half-expected him to scream, but the man didn't notice anything. Fallon didn't notice anything either; he waited for the heart to tell him something, but it seemed to be mute.

"Move your hand around a little," Caleb said in answer to Fallon's questioning glance. "Very few Cupids get the heart on the first try. Up a little, now left ... that should be it."

And it was. Fallon instantly knew, though he couldn't say how, exactly. It was like he was plugged in to the guy; he could feel what was in his heart, just like Caleb had said he would. It wasn't mind reading so much as emotion sensing, and it took Fallon a few moments to figure out which feelings were which.

"This is confusing," Fallon said. "I'm getting that he's open and not open to Jenny Lane at the same time."

"That's because the image on screen keeps changing," Caleb said. "Wait until Miss Lane is back on screen for more than a few seconds, then tell me what you find."

Fallon waited. The scene had switched to one with the male lead character, played by boy-band sensation Robbie Claine. Fallon groaned inwardly at having to wait for another Jenny scene, then chuckled at the thought of making the guy fall for Robbie. And that made him wonder something.

"Caleb?" he said. "If you're trying to get a guy and a girl together, and another guy gets in the way ... can you make two guys fall for each other?"

"Only if they are open to it," Caleb replied. "You're thinking of making this man fall for Mr. Claine?"

"Just wondering if it's possible," Fallon said. "I mean,

it just occurred to me, maybe when Cupids miss and make a guy fall for a guy … forget it."

"No, go on," Caleb said. "Ask your question."

"Well …" Fallon looked back to the screen to avoid Caleb's eyes. "I just wondered if that's where gay people come from."

There was a moment of uncomfortable silence between them, followed by another.

"Fallon," Caleb said at last, "does that make any sense to you?"

"Not really," Fallon replied.

"If a person isn't open to someone, they won't fall in love," Caleb said. "And that includes gays. You would know that if you'd paid attention to a word I've said."

"Sorry," Fallon muttered.

"And speaking of paying attention," he pointed at the screen, "Miss Lane is back."

Fallon, who'd been looking down at the floor, turned his head up. Jenny Lane was indeed on-screen, and the Japanese man thought she was a hottie.

"He's into her," Fallon said.

"Then give it to him," Caleb said. "Think of shooting Love from your fingertips into his heart, and it will happen. And do it now, before the scene changes again."

Fallon thought about firing Love into the man, and suddenly it happened. He felt the power flow from him into the guy, and it was quite a rush.

"Whoa," he said. He pulled his hand out of the man, who looked a lot more pleased to be there. "That was great."

"The first time always is," Caleb said with a smile. "Now you know how it is done. Choose someone else and try again."

Fallon did, several more times. Three guys and four girls, one of whom did prefer Jenny Lane over Claine. Caleb explained that the amount of Love Fallon gave out was in direct proportion to what was needed. The people in the audience got just enough to be starstruck, and Fallon could do several more before his supply of Love ran out.

"Now that you've had some practice," Caleb said, "let's go and try the real thing."

"Just one more," Fallon said, spying a middle-aged man sitting by himself in the front row.

"I'm not sure about that one," Caleb said, seeing where Fallon was going.

Fallon walked through the rows to the second aisle, knelt behind the man's seat, and reached his hand in. Immediately, he felt a huge dose of loneliness. When Jenny Lane appeared on screen, the feeling got worse. The man longed for her but felt completely unworthy.

"Yikes," Fallon said, pulling his hand out.

"I thought as much," Caleb said, walking up behind him. "What was it? Loneliness? Despair? Longing?"

"Yep," Fallon replied. "But I can make him happy if I find the right girl."

"No, you can't," Caleb replied. "He's been infected by

a Suicide, Fallon. That is why he feels so wretched. Most likely he came here thinking a romantic movie would cheer him up. Instead, it has had the opposite effect. And making him fall for Miss Lane will only make it worse."

"Why?"

"With a Suicide's taint on him," Caleb explained, "he's no good to himself, let alone anyone else. Have you ever had a very miserable person attracted to you?"

Fallon thought of Susan Sides, and nodded.

"You felt uncomfortable around her, didn't you?"

"Yes," Fallon said.

"That is how people feel when they are infected by Suicides," Caleb told him. "And love for Miss Lane will only create a deeper longing that can never be satisfied."

"Can't we do anything for him?" Fallon asked.

"No," Caleb replied. "He must overcome the Suicide's taint by himself. He is strong—he hasn't killed himself. But he has a long and difficult road ahead of him. There is, however, one important thing we can do," he added, rising to his feet.

"What's that?" Fallon asked.

"Suicides usually stay near their prey," Caleb explained, "so they can feed off the negative feelings. If we can find it and stop it, we can put this man out of his misery."

8

Fallon and Caleb searched the entire theater for the Suicide, but it was a lot more difficult than Fallon could have imagined. Their foe could walk through walls and hide inside solid objects, just as they could. They checked all the seats, and the floor around each audience member, but the Suicide was not to be found.

"That's enough," Caleb said after half an hour. "It's possible our presence may have frightened it off. But we have another hand to play."

"We do?" Fallon said.

"The movie is letting out," Caleb said, pointing to the crowd leaving the theater. "If we follow that man from a distance, we can catch the Suicide when it returns to him."

"How do you know it will?" Fallon asked.

"They always do," Caleb replied gravely. "It is in their nature."

They searched the crowd leaving the theater, and when the man didn't come out they hurried back inside. Fallon worried the man had killed himself in his seat, but it was nothing so drastic. He was simply one of those guys who sits through all the credits.

"Caleb?" Fallon asked. "What do we do when we find the Suicide?"

"We shower it with Love," Caleb told him. "That is what I did to the Suicide attacking you. You fire your Love like a spray all around it, neutralizing it."

"Neutralizing it," Fallon said. "Is that just a pretty way of saying we kill them?"

"They are already dead, Fallon," Caleb said, "just like us. And our power can render them helpless, just as the Suicide rendered you helpless."

"Oh," said Fallon. "So we just knock them out cold?"

"Enough Love," Caleb said, "will destroy their bodies, leaving only their souls behind. A Soul Reaper will then collect them and take them away."

"Is that what would have happened to me?" Fallon asked. "When that Suicide attacked me outside my house?"

"Not exactly," Caleb said. "Your body would have been destroyed, yes, but then your soul would have taken on the Suicide's aspect. You would have become one of them."

"Yikes," Fallon said.

"Ah," Caleb said, pointing. "He's leaving."

The man stood up and headed for the closest exit at the front of the theater. Fallon followed, but Caleb held him back at the exit door.

"Wait a moment," he said. "Then we'll follow. We'll have our best chance of catching the Suicide if we conceal our presence from it until the last possible second."

A moment or two later, they hurried through the door and found themselves on the top floor of a parking garage. The lot was roughly three-quarters full with cars, trucks, and SUVs—plenty of places for the Suicide to hide. Caleb crouched down inside the nearest car, then pulled Fallon in with him.

"Do you see it?" Caleb asked.

"No," said Fallon. "You?"

"Yes."

"What?" Fallon turned to his mentor. "Where?"

"Quiet," Caleb said. "We don't want it to know we are here. Watch that man. Look around him, and you'll see it."

Fallon looked hard, his eyes fixed on the depressed man as he unlocked the door of a maroon Honda. There didn't seem to be anything following him …

"I see it," Fallon said. "It's in the back of his car!"

"Very good," Caleb said. "Follow me. Quickly."

Caleb took off like a shot, and caught up to the man's Honda as he was pulling out of his parking space. Fallon lagged a meter or so behind and watched as Caleb fired a full burst of Love into the Honda's back seat.

The Suicide flew out the other side of the car and tumbled along the pavement. You're in for it now, Fallon mused as he got his first good look at a Suicide.

It was a person in a uniform, like him. It wasn't the same pink costume—the Suicide's one-piece outfit was a dark blue robe. As it stood back up, a shadowlike after-image followed its movements. It turned to face Fallon; a gray hood hid its face, but Fallon could tell it was staring at him.

"You again," it said. There was no hint, in its voice or appearance, what gender it was.

I nearly became one of those, Fallon thought. And then the words it had spoken sank in.

"What?" he said.

The Suicide leapt at him, but a blast of Love from Caleb's fingertips knocked it down.

"Never hesitate," Caleb said as he strode over to the Suicide and fired again. "They will take advantage of any opening."

"It knew me," Fallon said, watching as the Suicide crumbled under Caleb's onslaught.

"It's probably the same one that attacked you earlier today," Caleb said. "Possibly even the one who infected you during your life."

The Suicide disintegrated completely, and a dim gray blob of light rose up from the dust.

"Is that … ?"

" … its soul? Yes," Caleb said.

Fallon stared at the Suicide's soul, fascinated. He'd only caught a reflection of himself in this state. So this was the eternal part of every human being?

"It's kinda ugly," he said at last.

"You're not so hot yourself, jerkoff!" the Suicide replied, and Fallon jumped back. He'd forgotten souls could do that.

"It appears less attractive because of the harm it has caused," Caleb said.

"A karma thing?" Fallon asked, and Caleb nodded. "So, what do we do now? Do we go find a Soul Reaper?"

"One will be along soon," Caleb replied.

"How long do they usually … " Fallon asked.

"Move it," said Bud, elbowing him aside.

"That was quick," Caleb said.

"Yeah, well, I was in the area." Bud walked over to the soul. "You," he pointed at it. "Let's go."

"Charming as ever," Fallon said, watching as the Suicide's soul moved toward Bud the same way that he had done when he'd died.

"So." Bud turned to Fallon. "First day on the job and you've bagged yourself a Suicide. You probably think that'll earn you brownie points, right?"

"Not really," Fallon replied.

"Good," Bud replied, and he elbowed his way past

Fallon again. "Don't expect any. Ever." With that, Bud and the soul vanished into the ether.

"I violently dislike him," Fallon said, making a rude gesture at the spot where Bud had been.

"Don't think on it too much," Caleb told him. "Soul Reapers tend to be abrupt."

"Is there anyone nice on the other side?" Fallon asked.

"There's me," Caleb told him. "I'm pretty nice."

"Yeah, you're decent," Fallon conceded.

"If Louis were here," Caleb said, "he'd tell us to stop patting ourselves on the back and get to work."

"I'd just bet he would."

"But Louis isn't here," Caleb said. "What say we go catch a real man's movie?"

"Sounds good to me," Fallon said.

"You're going to do all right, Fallon," Caleb said as they walked back toward the mall. "I'm sure you'll make a fine Cupid."

"I hope so," Fallon replied. "I mean, what else am I going to do, right?"

"That's the spirit!"

They walked back through the exit door into the cinema and searched for a movie worth watching. As they did so, Fallon had a chance to reflect on the unusual turn his life—or rather, his death—had taken. He didn't like being forced into anything, but if he was completely honest with himself, he hadn't exactly loved the life he'd been leading before. He'd planned to graduate and go to college, but that was as far as he'd gotten. All he'd wanted from higher education was the chance to get away from his old life.

Here, in the afterlife, he had a chance to start over and do something truly great. He had it in his power to bring happiness to the world. All he had to do was learn how.

He also had the chance to fight off the forces that had led to his death. He could literally save lives. If he stopped only one more Suicide, the world would be the better for it.

What in the world could be better than that?

PART 2

9

Two weeks later, Fallon wasn't an expert Cupid but he was certainly more than competent. Under Caleb's careful monitoring, and thanks to his interest in poetry, Fallon had successfully put a couple together at a downtown Toronto pub during a spoken-word event. It wasn't a lot, but Caleb assured him it was more than most Cupids managed in that short time.

"Most new Cupids only manage to make one half of a couple fall in love," Caleb explained as they returned to the Cupid Center. "And then, the object of that person's affection leaves the area and is never seen again. Most new Cupids are rash that way, and end up with dozens of unrequited loves before they learn their chops. You, on the other hand, waited until you were sure your couple had a chance."

"Wasn't so hard," Fallon replied. "I mean, I checked both their hearts first … "

"Exactly!" Caleb said. "I am proud of you, Fallon."

His new body didn't blush, so Fallon simply nodded and said, "Thanks."

"Check up with them often," Caleb told him, "and see how their relationship develops. If you are lucky, and diligent, you might keep them going for a year or more."

"Only a year?"

"Well, they were very young," Caleb replied. "And youth is fickle. But you never know. Theirs might be true love. Wait and see."

They walked and chatted for half an hour as they made their way down the Love rows. Fallon seemed to know where he was going; Caleb had told him all Cupids could find their Love instinctively. He stopped in front of a small Love cube and knew right away that it was his.

"This is mine," he said, kneeling before the cube. It was no bigger than a lunchbox and looked like a clump of red snow, but to Fallon it was a trophy.

"Indeed it is," Caleb said. "Feast, my friend. You've earned it."

Fallon was way ahead of him. The taste was the same, only better. Somehow, the fact that it was his Love made it juicier, sweeter, and more satisfying.

"That better be your own this time."

Halfway through his second mouthful, Fallon turned to see who'd spoken. Then he groaned inwardly. It was Owen, the guy he'd stolen from after his Suicide attack.

Standing beside Owen, however, was a dark-skinned young woman. She had short hair and an athletic build, and Fallon guessed she was in the same age group as Owen and himself.

"Jada!" Caleb said, spreading his arms to embrace her. "How is my brightest student?"

"Just fine, Caleb," she replied, accepting the embrace. "Not too tight, now, you'll make Owen jealous."

Owen shot her a look but said nothing.

"Jada, this is Fallon," Caleb said, gesturing to him. "Fallon, this is ... "

"Your brightest student," Fallon finished for him.

"Don't take it personally," Jada said, offering her hand for a shake. "Caleb says that to all his students."

"Gotcha," Fallon said, and then he remembered something. "Wait a minute—Jada? Owen's girlfriend? From the car crash?"

"Fallon ... " Caleb said, and Owen glared daggers.

"That would be me, yeah," said Jada.

"Sorry," Fallon said. "That was a bit tactless, wasn't it? I just remembered Caleb telling me about it and ... "

"Caleb!" Owen said. "Are you telling everyone now?"

"He would have found out sooner or later," Caleb said, but he had the good grace to look sheepish.

"It's okay," Jada said with a shrug. "We're all dead here, and we all have our stories."

"What's yours?" Owen asked Fallon, and it was his turn to look sheepish.

"I, uh … tripped and fell off a bridge," he replied.

"Kinda clutzy, doncha think?" Owen said with a smirk.

"At least I wasn't drunk," Fallon shot back, and Owen's smirk became a sneer. Bull's-eye, Fallon thought, but he had no time to enjoy it; an electrical bolt made both of them jump.

"Havin' a little party here, are we?" Louis asked as he walked up to them. "Puttin' our feet up, takin' it easy?"

"No sir," Owen said, his body suddenly ramrod straight. "We … "

"You people got work," Louis said. "Socialize on your own time."

"When is that, exactly?" Jada asked.

Good question, Fallon thought. Cupids didn't need to sleep, and didn't get tired unless they were seriously low on Love. Nevertheless, some time off was needed, if only for the sake of morale.

"Time off comes when our karmic debt is paid," Owen said. "Right, sir?"

"Good man," Louis replied. "Get to it, people."

"You heard the man," Owen said, waving at Jada. "Let's go."

What a brown-noser, Fallon thought as Owen marched off.

"Bye, Caleb," Jada said, turning to follow Owen. "Nice to meet you, Fallon."

"Same here," Fallon replied. "See you…"

"What'd I just say? Party's over," Louis said. "That means you—"

"You must have heard the good news, Louis," Caleb interrupted cheerfully. "Fallon has done extremely well for—"

"Yeah, yeah, I'm putting him in the field," Louis said. "I got someone new for you to train. I'll bring him to ya later. Ricky, come with me."

"The name's Fallon."

"You're lucky I don't call you dirtbag!" Louis said.

"Louis, with all due respect, Fallon still needs another week's training," Caleb said. "All new Cupids get at least twenty days before…"

"Is everybody having hearing problems today?" Louis snapped. "You're reassigned, Caleb. So's he. End of story. Let's go, dirtbag." And he stomped off in the direction of the portals.

Caleb nodded reluctantly. "Good luck, Fallon. Come and find me if you need anything."

"Thanks, Caleb," Fallon said, then rushed to keep up with the boss. "So where am I going?" he asked, matching Louis's stride.

"A high school," Louis replied. "That'll be your entire

zone. I've got another couple of Cupids working the area around it. Your job will be the school, the kids, and the teachers."

"Okay," Fallon said. "But what if I need to leave the zone?"

"You won't."

"But if I need to follow a kid home, or to his job ... "

"You just don't know how to listen, do ya?" Louis said. "Your zone is the school. Everywhere else is someone else's responsibility. Got it?"

"Yes, sir," Fallon replied, offering a mock salute.

The electric blast hit him in the chest and knocked him off his feet. Two Cupids had to leap out of his way. One of them wasn't fast enough.

"Oof!" cried a middle-aged woman as Fallon slammed into her. They both went down, then she shoved Fallon off her.

"It's called respect," Louis said while the woman got back up. "Guess you've forgotten who's in charge here."

"I hadn't forgotten," Fallon said, swallowing his anger.

"Gonna say you're sorry to the lady ya hit?" It wasn't a question, or even a suggestion.

"I'm sorry," Fallon said to the woman. She nodded, then looked back at Louis.

She's afraid of him, Fallon realized. He looked around and saw every Cupid in the area desperately trying to mind his or her own business. They're all so damn afraid of him, Fallon thought. And there's nothing we can do about it. No union to report him to, no human resources to file a grievance with. Hell, they couldn't even quit.

"Let's go, kid," Louis said, and he turned and stomped off again.

Ten minutes later, they stepped through a portal onto the front lawn of a large high school. It was a modern-looking building, two floors high and two blocks wide. And it was green.

"Here ya are," Louis said, indicating the school. "Guildwood Mills High School. You stay inside those walls and do your work. Got it?"

"Absolutely," Fallon said, but Louis was already walking away. He held up a hand as he approached the sidewalk, opened a portal, and stepped through.

Fallon watched him go, then made a rude gesture at his back. It wasn't much, but it made him feel a tiny bit better. With that, he turned and headed into the school.

Inside, it was a high school. They were all the same to Fallon. He walked through a wide main hall filled with students eating their lunches in little groups. Straight ahead through the double doors would be an auditorium, and the main office would likely be located down the hall on the right. Fallon went left, and ended up in a hallway lined with lockers and classrooms. He knew he would find more of the same upstairs—lockers and classrooms and probably the library.

It was a typical, ordinary high school. And he was stuck there for God (or Louis) knew how long.

"At least it can't get worse," Fallon said, then smacked his head. He couldn't believe he'd just jinxed himself like that! He spun around, fully expecting to see Becky walking toward him. Highly unlikely, but just his luck, to be stuck in a school with the girl he loved. He'd probably have to make her fall for someone else. What torture that would be.

However, Becky was not walking toward him. Fate had chosen to be merciful. Fallon sighed, shook his head, and turned to continue down the hall.

And there she was, slumped against a locker, staring off into space. But it wasn't Becky. It was worse.

It was Susan Sides.

10

Fallon stood in the hallway of Guildwood Mills High School staring at the person who had almost driven him to suicide. She was sitting with her back against her locker door, unaware of his presence. For that, Fallon was extremely grateful.

As he watched her, the memories came flooding back. He remembered everything he'd given up so that he could be her friend; all the people he'd hung out with, all the good times he could have had. He'd lost Becky, and finally he'd lost his life.

And now, here she was. Fallon hoped she was just visiting, but he hadn't been having that kind of luck lately. He wanted to grab her, tell her to get the hell out of the school. The fact that he could not only made him more frustrated.

Fallon suddenly noticed she was looking at him. He took an involuntary step back. Could she see him? She frowned slightly, then turned away again. She hadn't seen him. He hoped.

As Fallon turned to leave, he saw a boy approaching from one of the classrooms, carrying an armload of books. When he saw Susan, his pace slowed noticeably.

"Oh hi, Ryan!" Susan said. "You're running a little late."

"You were waiting for me?" Ryan asked, stopping right in front of her.

"Yeah, you're just getting out of Chemistry, right?" Susan stood up. "I figured you'd come here to drop off your books and get your lunch, like you do every day. Guess you'd like to get to your locker, huh?" She stepped aside, and Ryan began working his combination lock.

She'd waited at his locker, Fallon thought, the way she used to do with me. And now she's going to ask why he's so late coming from class. And he's going to make up some lame excuse, like he wanted to talk to the teacher or something.

"So how come you're so late out of class?" Susan asked. "Usually you're pretty hungry, and you get here as soon as possible so you can get your lunch. And the Chemistry room's just over there."

"I was talking to Mr. Dewitzer about something,"

Ryan replied, slotting his books away on his locker's top shelf.

"Oh, like what?" Susan asked.

"Oh, just some stuff." Ryan pulled out a bag lunch and then slammed his locker closed.

"What kind of stuff?" Susan pressed.

"About the assignment," Ryan said, clicking his lock back into place. "Geez, why the Spanish Inquisition? It's not like we planned to meet up or anything."

"Sure we did," Susan said. "When I left you at your homeroom this morning, I said I'd see you at your locker at lunchtime. Don't you remember?"

Oh man, Fallon thought. She's sunk her claws in deep. I'll bet she's memorized his entire class schedule, so she can find him any time of the day. Just like she did with me.

Fallon watched as they walked off together, and felt helpless. He wanted to warn Ryan—if he didn't do something, Susan would drive him over the edge. Ryan looked about ready to jump off a bridge already. But what could he do?

He followed them back out into the main hall. When Susan had been his "friend," she'd eaten lunch with him in a small corner of his school's front foyer. At first, they'd sat and eaten with Fallon's friends. Then Susan had decided she didn't like his friends, and she'd asked if they could have lunch somewhere else, alone. Fallon hadn't wanted to, but Susan had been so damn persuasive.

"They don't understand me," she'd said. "They don't know how to listen, not like you do."

"But they're my friends," Fallon had said. "And Becky's my girlfriend. Why don't you at least try to ... "

"No," Susan had said. "Please come with me, Fallon. I don't want to be alone. I need to talk to someone right now, someone who will listen."

And so Fallon had left his friends for what he'd honestly thought would be one lunch period. He and Susan sat by the auditorium doors and he listened to her latest problem. The next day, when he left his last class before lunch, Susan intercepted him on his way to his locker.

"Wanna have lunch with me by the auditorium doors?" she'd said, ever so sweetly. And before he knew it, he was spending every lunch alone with her. His friends forgot about him.

Ryan and Susan sat down with a group of teens by the school's main entrance. Fallon hurried over and slipped into the wall behind them, and watched.

There were seven in the group, including Ryan and Susan. They sat in a small circle, their lunches in front of them, talking animatedly. There were three other girls and two guys, but to Fallon's eye there were no couples. Maybe he could do something about that later. For the moment, he wanted to keep an eye on Susan.

"We were just talking about God," said a long-haired brunette in a blue-collared blouse. "Any thoughts?"

"Don't tell me you're going all religious on us," Ryan said.

"We're not talking about religion," said a blond boy in black pants and a black shirt. "Cynthia's doing a project for her sociology class."

"I want to get as many opinions as possible," the long-haired brunette said.

"Why don't you talk to the Psalm Troupe?" Ryan asked with a chuckle.

"I think it's pretty obvious what they would say," said a plain-looking girl in a faded blouse and worn jeans.

"Yeah, plus they creep me out," Cynthia added.

"They have a new pamphlet out," said a short-haired boy with glasses. He pulled a small leaflet from the breast pocket of his checkered shirt and read with mock seriousness. "*Gary thought no one knew about his alternative lifestyle, but someone was watching!*"

"Are they still picking on gays?" said the girl in the faded clothing.

"As if they'll ever stop," said Cynthia. "Right, Peter?"

"Wait, this gets better!" the checkered-shirt boy said, skipping to the end. "*On the Last Day as he stood trembling before God, he found he could not hide…*" He paused for drama. "*…from Judgment!*"

They laughed then, all but Susan. She shifted uncomfortably, just enough for Ryan to notice.

"I'm sure God isn't like that," said a blond girl in a tie-dyed T-shirt. "I'm with Trina on this one. Universal force for good."

"Thanks, Lucy," said the girl in faded clothing, offering a shy smile. She played absently with her shoulder-length hair.

"So I've heard from everyone except you two," Cynthia said, pointing at Ryan and Susan. "What've you got for me?"

Before Ryan could answer, Susan picked up her lunch and stood up.

"I ... have to go," she said, and she turned and walked away quickly.

"Oh, man," said Ryan.

"Did we offend her?" asked Lucy.

"Like that'd be hard," muttered the blond boy in black pants.

"Brad!" said Lucy. "That's not nice."

"Maybe," the blond boy replied. "But it's true."

"I'd better go check on her," Ryan said, rising slowly to his feet.

"No!" Fallon jumped up and stepped in front of him. "No, you stay here if you know what's good for you!" He automatically held up his hands to block Ryan, then remembered he was insubstantial in this world.

"Who said that?" Trina asked, her head snapping up.

"Who said what?" Ryan asked, stopping.

"That's right, stay here," Fallon said. "Do not go with that human leech."

"There it is again!" said Trina. "A voice! He called Susan a leech."

"What?" said Fallon, turning to look at her.

"Come on, who said that?" Trina glanced from friend to friend.

"I didn't," said Peter.

"Wasn't me," said Brad.

"Trina, are you hearing things again?" Cynthia asked.

Oh yes she is, Fallon thought. She heard me loud and clear. This could be useful.

And Ryan stayed! He sat back down again, though he did look nervously in the direction Susan had gone. Maybe my comments actually reached him, Fallon thought. Or maybe Ryan's just better at denying her than I was. Either way, he might just stand a chance.

11

Fallon remained with the group of teens for the rest of the lunch hour, but he said no more. He didn't want to freak the girl out, not if he was going to ask for her help later.

From what he could gather from the group, this wasn't the first time Trina had heard voices. First she'd confided only in Cynthia, then the rest of them.

Fallon also learned that the group didn't much like Susan, either.

"Don't know who your invisible guy is, Trina," said Peter, "but he got Susan's number, all right."

"Totally," added Brad.

"You guys..." said Lucy, but only half-heartedly.

"She has a lot of problems," Ryan said. "She doesn't make friends easily."

She told you that too, did she? Fallon thought.

"Remember," Ryan added, "she only transferred here a couple weeks ago. She wanted to get away from her old school because her best friend there committed suicide."

"Oh," Brad said. "Oh, man."

"That poor girl," Cynthia added.

So that's why she's here, Fallon thought. I wonder who that friend was, who killed himself? The only person she was friends with was … oh, right.

"So, Trina," Peter asked, "is that voice guy still around?" He said it with what Fallon knew to be a patronizing smile. Not a believer, it seemed.

"I can't hear anything," Trina said. "Look, I'm sorry I mentioned it. Let's talk about something else, okay?"

They did. Fallon watched them, and as he did so he made contact with their hearts. No sense wasting a good opportunity, right? He checked out Peter first, and learned he had a thing for Lucy. She was sitting next to him, which was a good sign, but when Fallon touched Lucy's heart he found no interest for Peter. Indeed, she didn't seem interested in anyone in the group.

Fallon moved on. Brad was open to Cynthia or Lucy, but not Trina. Ryan could be paired with all three girls, and Cynthia was open to the entire group. Trina …

Fallon hesitated. If she could hear his voice, she might feel his hand. He would wait before he tried her.

The bell rang, and all around the main foyer students got up and headed for their classes. Trina, Cynthia, and Ryan went down the left corridor, and the others went right. Fallon followed Trina, hoping to catch her alone. It was luck, then, that they were with Ryan. Fallon could have smacked himself for not guessing who'd be waiting at his locker.

"Hi, guys!" Susan said, all smiles and cheeriness. Fallon knew that for the act it was. As soon as Susan got Ryan alone, she'd want to know why he didn't come after her. And she would not be happy about it.

"Just keep right on walking," he said, touching Ryan's heart again. It didn't work, but Fallon hadn't really expected it to.

"Everything all right?" Cynthia asked Susan as they stopped by Ryan's locker.

"Yeah, everything's peachy," Susan said. "I just need to talk to Ryan about something before we go to class."

Ryan looked back at Cynthia and Trina, his eyes pleading.

"We'll catch you later, Ryan," Cynthia said.

"Don't leave him alone with her," Fallon implored, speaking right into Trina's ear. His voice visibly startled her, but she quickly regained her composure.

"Bye Ryan, Susan," she said, and walked quickly after Cynthia.

"Oh, come on!" Fallon called after them, but if Trina heard, she didn't show it.

"You've got English now, right?" Susan asked while Ryan opened his locker. "I'll walk you there. My class is on the way."

"What did you want to talk to me about?" Ryan asked as he sorted through his schoolbooks.

"Well, I ... " Susan said. "I just wondered if you were mad at me."

"You bet he is," Fallon said, but Ryan said no.

"It's just that you didn't come after me when I left the group earlier," Susan said. "When you didn't, I figured you must be mad at me."

"I'm not mad at you, Susan," Ryan said. "I just wanted to stick with my friends."

"So I'm not your friend?" Susan asked.

"No! That's not what I'm saying," Ryan told her.

"If a friend of mine walked away," Susan said, "I would have gone to see what was wrong. I'm not saying I'm mad at you for not doing it, I'm just saying what I'd do."

"I'm sorry, Susan, okay?" Ryan slumped down against his locker. His face said he wasn't going anywhere for a while, and he knew it.

"So you'll come next time?" Susan said, sitting down beside him.

"Yes," said Ryan helplessly.

"Thank you," Susan said, and she took his hand and squeezed it in both of hers. "You're a true friend."

Fallon turned and walked away. He couldn't take any

more, and there was nothing he could do. Susan had her claws in him, and Fallon knew Ryan would need help to pull those claws out.

And that help was going to come from Trina, whether she liked it or not.

It took Fallon a while to find Trina. Guildwood Mills had a lot of classrooms, each one packed with students. Fallon's ability to walk through walls, however, made his search much easier.

Finally, in a French class on the school's southwest side, he hit pay dirt. Trina was sitting in the middle of the first row, next to the wall. Fallon slipped into that wall and sidled up to her, then squatted beside her desk.

Trina, who had been slouching in her chair, sat up suddenly. She knows I'm here, Fallon thought.

"Hello, Trina," he said. "I want to talk to you."

She slowly turned her head to look, and for a moment Fallon thought she could actually see him. Then he realized she couldn't; her eyes found nothing to focus on, and she turned back to the front of the class.

"I'm not going to hurt you," Fallon said. He wanted to put her at ease, and that seemed a good place to start.

"Who are you?" she whispered.

"Call me Fallon," he told her. "I'm a Cupid."

Her eyebrow wrinkled. "A what?"

"A Cupid," Fallon explained. "I make people fall in love. People can't see or hear us, but I know you can hear me. And I need your help."

"Go away," Trina hissed. "Leave me alone."

"Sorry, no can do," Fallon said. "Your friend Ryan is in trouble. I need you to ... "

"Go away!" she said, and pounded her fist on the wall, right through Fallon's face.

"Is there something wrong, Miss Porten?" asked the teacher, a middle-aged man in a tweed jacket and a bad comb-over.

"No, Mr. Londry," Trina replied, blushing as half the class turned to look at her. "Just ... thinking of something."

"Oh," Mr. Londry said. "Well, ah, perhaps you could think about paying attention? Ha, ha."

"Oh dear," Fallon said. "He thinks he's funny." If the class thought the same, they didn't show it.

"I will, Mr. Londry," Trina replied. "Sorry."

Trina's classmates turned away, and Mr. Londry returned to the blackboard. Fallon waited a few moments more, then tried again.

"That wasn't nice," he said. "Your fist went through my head."

Trina wrote something on a blank page in her notebook, then turned it to the wall. Fallon read it. It said: *Good.*

"Ha, ha, I'm glad you're happy," Fallon said. "Now listen up. I'm not going anywhere, not until you agree to help me out."

I'm in class.

"So what?" Fallon said. "It's only French class."

I have a study period next I will listen then.

"All right," Fallon said. "Study period it is. What classroom?"

218.

"Okay, see you there," Fallon said. "Don't stand me up. This is important."

I won't.

Fallon backed off. As he did so, he watched Trina's shoulders relax. He had no doubt she was scared of him, and he didn't want to frighten her, but he didn't think he could help it. For all intents and purposes, he was a ghost. If he didn't put her at ease, her fear might get the better of her, and she might not help him.

He could force her, of course. He could scream in her ears until she went insane, or sing badly until the annoyance got to her. Fallon didn't want to force her—that wasn't his style. But if it came to it, he would do what he had to.

He walked to the back of the class, and waited.

12

Fallon passed the time until the end of class checking the hearts of the students. Very few were able to listen to the teacher for any length of time, so Fallon got a good idea of who was interested in whom.

The results, however, were less than inspiring. Several boys liked the hot blonde at the back of the class, but she never looked their way. The two pretty boys near the window got a lot of interest from girls, but their eyes didn't roam nearly enough to make a connection.

And nobody seemed interested in Trina. Poor girl, Fallon thought. Then again, it was only one classroom. Hardly a cross-section of the school.

One of the students had a crush on Mr. Londry. What does she see in him, Fallon wondered. The teacher wasn't the most boring person he'd ever known, but he was in the top ten. Maybe the last Cupid to work this zone had a weird sense of humor. Or maybe student crushes on teachers were evidence of more Cupid practice runs, like the movie star crushes had been. Fallon made a mental note to find the girl someone else to focus on as soon as possible.

As French class let out, Fallon followed Trina down the hall. He tried to keep his distance; she could sense him, and he didn't want her any more freaked out than she was.

When she headed into the stairwell, however, Fallon realized he might have a problem. She's going to room 218, he remembered, and he looked around for someone going in the same direction. Luckily there were lots of students heading upstairs to their next class; Fallon reached into a boy's back, touched his heart, and got a free ride up to the second floor. Two steps later, he let go, then walked quickly to catch up with Trina.

"Hey, spirit girl!"

Fallon looked left and saw a small group of girls gathered around a locker. When Trina looked at them, they waggled their fingers beside their heads and said, "Wooo!"

Trina turned away sharply and walked faster. The girls laughed at her back, and one of them called "Spirit girl!" again.

Oh, man, Fallon thought. Not exactly popular, is she?

Room 218 was at the end of the hall, near the entrance to the library. Trina hurried in and took a seat in the same position as in her last class—in the middle and against the wall. The class was about half full of students, most of whom sat near the back. There was plenty of space around Trina; their conversation would be undisturbed. The teacher at the front had her nose buried in a Harlequin; she wouldn't interfere, either.

"Hello again, Trina," Fallon said, standing in the wall beside her.

Hello, she wrote back. *Who are you? What do you want with me?*

"I told you, my name is Fallon," he said. "I'm a Cupid. I make people fall in love."

Seriously?

"Yeah, didn't really believe it either, not at first," Fallon said. "Look, you're still kind of freaked out, right?"

Yes.

"Okay then," Fallon said. "I'll tell you about myself and what I'm doing here. If you know me better, you'll see I'm nothing to be scared of."

Okay.

"Right," Fallon said, and he began.

It took him only ten minutes to tell Trina about his death and rebirth. She listened without saying (or writing) anything, and when he was finished, Fallon had to wonder if she'd paid any attention at all.

Louis sounds like a real jerk, she wrote, putting Fallon's fears to rest.

"He sure is," he replied. "Well, is there anything you want to ask me?"

Plenty, she wrote. *How do you make people fall in love? Wait, I have another question first. What is your problem with Susan?*

"That," Fallon said with a sigh, "is a long story."

I have half an hour left. Tell me.

Fallon walked through her desk and sat on the floor beside it. He'd known he would have to tell her, but that didn't make it any easier for him.

"She's the reason I wanted to kill myself," he said, and he told her about Susan Sides. It took another ten minutes, starting with the time he first met her and finishing with the events of that fateful, awful day.

"I don't know if she does it on purpose," Fallon said, "but that doesn't stop the effect she has on people. That's why I need your help, Trina. We've got to get Ryan away from her."

He looked up to see if Trina had a response. She was looking in his direction; she must have sensed his shift in position.

"I'm so sorry," she whispered.

"Thanks," Fallon said. "You're a great listener."

She smiled at that, a really pretty smile.

I'm going to make someone love that smile, he thought.

"I'll talk to Susan," Trina whispered. "Maybe I can get her to see the counselor."

"She won't go," Fallon told her. "Trust me on this. I

tried, but she wouldn't do it. All she wanted was to suck the life out of me."

"You make her sound like one of those Suicides," Trina said.

"Yeah," Fallon said. "Who needs Suicides when you've got Susan Sides?"

Fallon started to chuckle, but then his eyes went wide. Suicides. Susan Sides. That had to be more than just a coincidence. Now that he thought about it, Susan fit the profile of a Suicide to a T.

But how? Suicides were dead, weren't they?

"Fallon?" Trina said.

If it was at all possible that Susan was a Suicide, Louis would know. Fallon really didn't want to talk to the man, but he had to find out. And it was probably his duty to report it, though that had never been specified in his training.

"I've got to go, Trina," he told her. "Don't try to talk to her, it might be dangerous. When I get back, you've got to help me save Ryan."

Fallon ran out of the classroom, then held up his hands and created a portal to the Cupid Center. He hurried through and went in search of his boss.

But he quickly realized that the search was hopeless. The Cupid Center was huge; Louis could be anywhere inside it. He might not even be there at all, and there was no way to check. All Fallon could do was run around the Cupid Center and hope to get lucky.

"Not a very good system," he said. Then he thought of how quickly Louis had come when he'd eaten from another Cupid's Love cube. Louis must manage thousands if not millions of Cupids, yet he'd turned up almost instantly. Had something alerted him?

Fallon decided to find out. He walked over to the nearest desk-sized Love cube, broke a piece off, and waited. If he was right, he would not need to eat it. He didn't want to steal from another Cupid, even one with a cube as large as this one.

He tossed the piece of Love in the air and caught it a few times. On the seventh toss he missed, because a blast of electricity zapped him in the back.

"Just don't learn, do ya?" Louis said, striding quickly toward him.

Well, it worked, Fallon thought.

"You are not allowed to eat another Cupid's Love!" Louis went on. "Thought I made that clear the last time."

"I didn't eat any," Fallon said. "I was …"

"I don't like liars," Louis said, giving Fallon another shock.

"I was trying to find you!" Fallon screamed through clenched teeth.

"Well, ya found me," Louis said. "Now we're gonna go and take some Love of yours to replace what you stole."

"But I have the piece I took right here," Fallon said, picking it up and showing Louis. "I only took it because I thought it would make you come. Look, I'm putting it back…" He tried to do just that, but another jolt knocked it out of his hand.

"It's been on the floor," Louis pointed out. "Would you eat it?" To drive his point home, he stepped on the dropped Love and squashed it. "We're taking some of your Love, end of story. Let's go."

"Fine," Fallon said with barely contained anger. "But I need to talk to you about something."

"Talk on the way." Louis was already walking off.

"I need to talk about Suicides," Fallon said as he caught up. "Can they take on a human form?"

"No," Louis said.

"Can they possess someone?"

"No."

"It's just that there's this girl in that school who acts a lot like…"

"You having hearing problems?" Louis said, stopping in front of him. "I said no. Suicides are dark spirits. They don't take on physical form, and they can't possess people. You got that?"

"Yes," Fallon said.

"Good." Louis turned and started walking again.

"If I have any more questions," Fallon asked, "how do I find you?"

"You don't," Louis said. "You were trained. You shouldn't have any questions."

"Uh huh," Fallon said.

He realized he'd made a mistake. He didn't believe

a word Louis had said—in fact, Fallon was more certain now that Susan was a Suicide than he'd been before Louis told him it was impossible.

If Louis wouldn't make time for him, there was only one other Cupid he knew who could help him—Caleb. The question now was, where was Caleb and how could he find him? Unfortunately, Fallon realized, the only person who knew that was Louis.

This was not going to be easy.

13

Fallon guessed it was at least an hour before he got back to the portals. The design of the Cupid Center was all wrong; if it had been up to him, there would be a portal next to every Love cube so that Cupids could avoid all the unnecessary walking time.

And time was of the essence. If he wanted to reconnect with Trina, Fallon knew he needed to get back to Guildwood Mills before the school day ended.

He was very annoyed, and not just about the lost time. Louis had taken half of the Love he had left, far more than the tiny chunk Fallon had broken off the other cube. Injustice piled on top of injustice, with zero accountability.

"No," Fallon told himself. He'd decided not to let Louis rile him, since the man clearly enjoyed it. He would stay calm and deal with it as best he could until he found a way to take Louis down a peg.

In the meantime, he had a job to do. Fallon chose a portal and went through it, returning to Guildwood Mills' front entrance.

Trina's study period would be long since finished. Fallon knew he'd have to find her again, and that could take a while. He also had to get a couple together, too—his Love cube wasn't going to grow by itself.

And he had to find Susan and see what she was up to. Amazingly, he didn't have to wait long to find out.

Susan Sides stood by herself across the hall from the boys' bathroom. Classes were in session and the halls were empty; she had no reason to be there.

Of course, Fallon knew immediately who she was waiting for. He ducked through the wall into the boys' room and found Ryan, staring at the mirror above the sinks. He did not look good: he was leaning on the sink for support, and his features bore an expression of helplessness.

It hadn't been so long ago, Fallon reflected, that he'd been hiding from Susan in the boys' room. He'd sat in a stall for twenty minutes, and when he finally left, Susan had still been waiting for him. Now Ryan was on that same sinking boat.

Tentatively, knowing what he would find, Fallon reached a hand into Ryan's chest. Instantly, he felt a wave of hopelessness; Ryan had been infected with depression.

"Hang in there, dude," Fallon said, and he turned and walked back through the wall.

Susan was still there. She didn't look impatient or bored, just resolute. She would wait all day, if necessary.

Fallon raised his hands and gave her a blast of Love. If he was right and she was a Suicide, the Love would finish her.

However, it did not. She stood against the wall the same as before, unaware that anything had happened.

Fallon saw two possibilities. One, he was wrong and Susan was just a very annoying and clingy person. Two, he was right and Susan was a Suicide, but being human shielded her from the Love. If he was right, his job had just become a lot harder.

There was a way to be sure. When the other Suicide had attacked him, Fallon had felt misery more powerful than he could have imagined. Caleb had warned him not to let a Suicide touch him, because the effect would be the same.

If I touch her, he thought, and she is a Suicide, I'll feel the misery.

It was a plan that would work, but with one serious drawback. The depression would overtake him, and there wasn't anyone around who could help him. If he were to survive, he'd need a major dose of Love to get him through it.

That meant he had to get to work. He had to replenish his Love supply or he wouldn't be useful to anyone.

Behind him, the boys' room door opened and Ryan stepped out. He did not look surprised to see Susan waiting for him. Rather, he looked resigned.

"There you are!" Susan said. "I thought maybe you'd fallen in. You feeling sick?"

"No, I'm okay," Ryan replied, though his face said the opposite.

"It's just you were in there for half an hour," Susan said. "I thought that maybe you were hiding from me."

"No! Why would you think that?" Ryan said.

"Oh, no reason," Susan said. "It's just that you were in there for so long, and we missed half of math class, so if you're not sick, then what were you doing?"

"Just … using the bathroom," Ryan said. "I didn't think you were going to wait for me."

"Of course I was going to wait for you," she said. "You're my best friend."

Fallon turned and walked away. There was nothing he could do for Ryan, not yet.

Three classrooms later, Fallon finally found a couple he could match up. It hadn't been easy—a large number of students were actually paying attention to their teachers. Luckily, there were still some at the back of each class who roamed their eyes around.

In a Geography class, Fallon hit pay dirt. A dark-skinned girl sitting by the window kept checking out an Asian boy at the front. It would have been easy to make her fall for him, but Fallon wanted to be sure the guy was willing, too. He walked over to the guy's desk and slid his hand into his heart, then whispered:

"Turn around. Check her out."

The guy did, and Fallon immediately felt an attraction. He wasted no time firing Love into the guy's heart; a few seconds later, he had the girl's heart, too. They stared at each other across the classroom, lost in the other's eyes.

"Yeah!" Fallon said, pumping his arm. He'd done it again.

"Jason, Penny, are you two in love?"

Fallon groaned inwardly and watched as the red-faced teens turned to face the teacher. That, Fallon realized, would be a continuing problem if he brought couples together in classrooms.

"Sorry, Miss Mitchell," Jason said sheepishly.

"If you can tear your eyes off each other for a few moments," Miss Mitchell said with a smile, "we were discussing erosion as it relates to the current state of the Canadian Shield. Any thoughts?"

Fallon mouthed an apology to Jason and Penny and turned to leave. After he'd left the room, he could still feel the two teens' hearts. He'd had a similar experience with the first couple he'd brought together, at the poetry event—he could still sense where they were, and what their feelings were, too. That was important; he'd have to check in on them several times to keep their love flowing.

Fallon walked across the main foyer, looking for another set of classrooms. The foyer was currently empty;

classes were still in full swing. Fallon walked straight through the wall at the far end, expecting to end up in the middle of another classroom.

He stopped. Did a double take. This wasn't a classroom. Not unless it was Biology and they took anatomy very seriously.

He was in the shower area of the girls' changing room. There were seven girls in there with him, all naked, most of them showering while others toweled themselves off by the doorway.

Fallon knew the decent thing to do was cover his eyes and retreat through the wall behind him. But how often did life, or death, give you an opportunity like this?

"I am such a perv," he said, unable to look away. He'd had no contact with female nudity in all of his seventeen years, not counting the porn magazines he'd flipped through. He'd hoped he might get there with Becky, but Susan's invasion of his life had ruined those plans.

Susan, he thought, reminding himself of what he was supposed to be doing. He could look at naked girls later. Right now, he had to find...

"Trina!" he said, as she walked through the door wearing only a towel.

Trina froze. Her eyes went wide. And her towel chose that moment to drop.

"Oops," Fallon said.

This was going to be awkward.

14

Fallon, you jerk!" Trina cried, covering herself with her arms while simultaneously reaching down for her towel. "Get out of here, you sicko!"

"I'm so sorry!" Fallon slapped a hand over his eyes at last. "I was just... I mean, I didn't know this was... "

"Get out!" Trina screamed, snatching up her towel and wrapping herself up in one swift motion. Then she turned and bolted from the shower room.

"What's her problem?" one of the girls asked, turning off her shower and reaching for a towel.

"Haven't you heard?" said another as she rinsed conditioner from her blond hair. "She sees dead people."

"You mean like the kid in that movie?" asked a Japanese girl.

"That's what she says," said the blonde. "I say she's a freak."

"Oh, that's original," Fallon said. He knew he should leave, but he had to try and straighten things out. He had the distinct impression that Trina was not part of the in crowd. And he'd just made things worse.

He crossed the shower room and entered the changing room, keeping his hand over his eyes and taking quick peeks to see where he was going. There were a few girls in the room in various states of undress, and Fallon tried very hard not to look at them.

Trina was standing alone in the corner, already half dressed. Fallon approached slowly, trying to think of how to apologize.

"Go away," she said without turning, as she threw on her shirt.

"I'm not looking," Fallon said. "I'm really sorry. I was in there by accident, I swear."

"Oh, bull!" Trina said, turning to face the sound of his voice. "You just 'accidentally' ended up in a room full of naked teenage girls?"

"Who's she talking to?" a girl asked.

"Keep your voice down!" Fallon said. "The other girls think you're nuts."

"They ... do not," Trina said, suddenly aware of how many eyes were on her.

"I was just ... " she said to them, then turned around awkwardly and sat down on a bench. The other girls stared a few moments longer, then went back to their hushed whispers.

"Freak," one whisperer said, just loud enough.

"Look." Fallon squatted next to the bench. "It was stupid of me to go in there. I wasn't thinking."

Trina said nothing. Which, Fallon thought, was probably for the best. He stood up and turned to leave, and that was when he saw the seven girls from the showers standing there. They were still naked and carried their towels in their hands.

"Hey, Trina!" the blond one said, and all seven girls threw their towels over their heads like ghostly hoods.

Trina made the mistake of looking. All seven girls shook their towels and went, "Oooooh!" like B-movie phantoms.

Trina stood up, pushed her way through them and ran for the doorway. The girls laughed, and Fallon made a mental note to deny them love for as long as they lived.

He chased after Trina, but he didn't have to go far. A large gorilla in a tracksuit—the gym teacher, Fallon guessed—had stopped her at the changing room doors.

"This hair looks dry," the gorilla said, grabbing a handful of Trina's hair. "Did you shower?"

"I don't have time, Miss Labonski," Trina said. "I have to get to my next class."

"You know the rules," the gym teacher said. "Back you go. Take your shower."

"But ... " Trina protested.

"Go!" Miss Labonski barked, and Trina went back in.

Fallon made a rude gesture at the gym teacher's face, then turned and followed Trina.

All the girls went silent as Trina re-entered the changing room. As soon as she reached her spot in the far corner, the hushed whispers continued.

"I didn't mean for this to happen," Fallon told her.

"Skip it," she mumbled back. "It's just high school."

The other girls finished changing and began filing out. Trina undressed slowly, waiting for the others to leave.

"I'm gonna go," Fallon told her. "I don't want to embarrass you any further. I do need to talk to you, though. Can you meet me later?"

"Sure," she said. "Meet me after school."

"You got it," Fallon said, and he left the changing room. He was halfway across the gym when he saw one of the other girls talking with a beefy jock in shorts and a T-shirt. More boys came from the changing room across the gym—clearly it was time for their Phys Ed class.

Fallon approached the girl and boy. She'd been one of Trina's tormentors and didn't deserve what he was about to do, but Fallon needed more Love and this was too good to pass up. He put his hands into their hearts and felt mutual interest. Perfect. He zapped them both, and smiled when their eyes widened ever so slightly.

"To the happy couple!" Fallon cried, raising a mock glass in a toast to the rest of the gym.

Which was why he saw the black form slithering into the girls' changing room.

"Suicide!" Fallon cried, and charged after it. There was an already very miserable girl in the changing room.

Fallon ran through the wall in time to see the Suicide enter the showers. Terrific, he thought, but he knew he could not stop.

Trina was standing under a nozzle at the room's far end. The Suicide made straight for her, and Trina spun around and covered up.

She senses us, Fallon thought as he closed in on his prey.

"Trina, it's a Suicide!" he yelled. "Duck!"

Trina ducked. The Suicide spun around and had just enough time to register surprise before Fallon plowed into it, driving it over Trina's head and through the wall.

He immediately realized his mistake. A physical attack on a Suicide was stupid; any contact with it would only harm himself. He could feel the cold hand of despair clutching his soul even as he shoved the dark creature away.

They landed in the school's main lobby on the other side of the wall. The Suicide regained its feet first; Fallon was slowed down by depression. The creature lunged for him, but Fallon got his hands up in time.

"Back off!" he shouted, blasting the Suicide with a full burst of Love. The creature fell back and Fallon managed a smile. He was going to kick this thing's ass!

And then his Love ran out. Fallon felt the most intense hunger of his life and afterlife, even as his fingers stopped their barrage. He also felt exhausted, in no shape whatsoever to continue the fight.

The Suicide, who had thrown its arms up in a defensive posture, lowered them slowly. Then it smiled.

It knows, Fallon thought. And he turned to run.

15

Fallon ran across the school's main foyer, the Suicide right behind him. His only hope was to get back to the Cupid Center, where the Suicide wouldn't be able to follow. Then he could eat some Love and come back to kick its depression-sowing butt.

If he made it back.

Fallon raised his hand and was halfway through opening the portal when the Suicide caught him. He fell to the floor, the dark creature on his back, trying to fight it off. It was hopeless; for every second the Suicide remained attached to him, Fallon's will slipped away. Deep sadness filled him, made him weak.

I'm done, Fallon thought. He was dying a second time, and this time felt worse. He realized he'd gotten to like being a Cupid, even thought he was getting good at it. Now he'd never know how good he might have been …

Something slammed into them, flinging both Fallon and the Suicide backward across the foyer. Fallon landed on his back and his head fell to the right, so he was able to see two Cupids running toward him.

I've been rescued, he thought. Yay. Fallon thought he should be more excited, but the attack had left him emotionally numb.

One of the Cupids leapt over Fallon and chased after the Suicide. The second one stopped and knelt at Fallon's side. He recognized him; it was Owen, who he'd stolen from the last time a Suicide had attacked him.

"Are you okay?" Owen asked, looking at Fallon closely. "Oh, it's you."

"Hi, Owen," Fallon replied without enthusiasm. "Thanks for the rescue."

"You can thank Jada for that," Owen said, all concern gone from his face. "Can you move?"

"I don't know," Fallon said.

"Get yourself back and eat some Love," Owen said. "We've got a Suicide to catch."

He ran off and vanished through the nearest wall. Fallon tried to get up, then lay back down again.

Lying down felt good. His Cupid body didn't need to sleep, but Fallon had fond memories of slumber and felt sure a good rest would solve all his problems. Unless Louis came and saw him. Boy, he'd really tear him a new one! It wouldn't matter to him at all that Fallon was the victim of a Suicide…

Fallon struggled, groaned, forced himself to sit up. He felt knocked out because of a Suicide, he wanted to sleep because of a Suicide, and he'd died because of a Suicide. He'd be damned if he'd let a Suicide have the last laugh.

Of course, that was easier said than done. He tried to stand but could not, so he started crawling. It wasn't as hard as he'd feared, and gave him the first glimmerings of hope.

And then, someone stepped in him. The foot landed squarely in his back; the walker stopped suddenly, and Fallon felt the familiar feelings of gloom overtaking him.

It's the Suicide, he thought, looking over his shoulder. It *wasn't* the Suicide, he noted with wide-eyed shock.

It was Susan Sides.

"No…" Fallon gasped.

She looked down at him. She squinted at first, but then her eyes widened. She smiled. There was recognition in her eyes, and not a little bit of pleasure.

She remembers me, Fallon thought, and he tried to crawl away. It was like dragging a sack of bricks through glue now, and the despair was getting worse. Still, he managed to pull himself away from her foot, and as soon as he did, the depression flow stopped.

But Susan was on to him now. She took another step and planted both feet through him, and Fallon lost the ability to move.

She had him. And she was going to destroy him again. Fallon felt his world dropping off, the way he'd dropped off the Pape Street Bridge that fateful day. He felt as if he were tumbling down a dark hole, or perhaps the world was falling up and away, stranding him in blackness. He couldn't move, couldn't speak, could barely think, and hope and happiness were gone forever...

"Young lady! What are you doing out of class?"

Fallon's closed eyes were too heavy to open, but he heard loud footsteps approaching. He couldn't believe his luck; someone had caught Susan skipping!

"I was just going to the bathroom, Mr. Mehta," Susan said.

"You and I both know that's nowhere around here," Mr. Mehta said, his lightly accented voice sounding more amused than off-put. "Come on now, your principal wasn't born yesterday, you know. Where are you supposed to be?"

"English class," Susan said.

Just take her away, Fallon thought.

"Then that is where you need to be," Mr. Mehta said. "Come along now."

"But I..." Susan began, staring down at Fallon. "I was..."

"I can't have students roaming the hallways during class time," Mr. Mehta said as he gently but firmly led Susan away. "If I did, you wouldn't learn anything, and then where would we be?"

Susan cast one last glance over her shoulder at Fallon, giving him a look that promised things between them weren't over. At that point, Fallon couldn't have cared less. Emotionally he was a non-entity, and his mind was almost numb. He lay unmoving on the floor, his eyes fixed on the corridor Susan and the principal had gone down, and his world was nothing except the images he saw. He took in every detail of the hallway doors, of the walls around it, of the soft drink dispenser next to them. However, none of those details mattered in the slightest.

A tiny part of him wondered if he was still alive.

Time passed. How much, he couldn't be certain. Eventually he saw a pair of pink-clad feet appear in front of him, then another pair; Owen and Jada, he guessed. The two Cupids talked, and the feet walked out of his view just before he felt hands lifting him in the air. Owen and Jada slung Fallon's arms over their shoulders and began walking forward. Fallon's head faced downward and his neck had no strength, so all he saw was floor.

They left the school, and then they were back in the Cupid Center; Fallon saw the pavement of the school walkway change to the familiar white flooring. That flooring went by for a short while, then they crossed a threshold into a room.

A new pair of hands took hold of Fallon and guided him gently down onto a small platform a meter off the floor. Fallon found himself looking up as he was laid down on his back. He saw Jada's face, looking down on him with genuine concern. Owen stood next to her, staring down at him with disdain.

What's his problem, Fallon wondered, before realizing he really didn't care.

A new face entered his field of vision, an old yet wise face that regarded him kindly. He's my friend, Fallon thought, then realized he didn't care about that, either.

The man with the kind face went away. Jada said something to him and took her hand off his arm—Fallon didn't remember her placing her hand there—then she too turned and left. Owen was long gone.

He lay there, staring at the ceiling, thinking of nothing. And time began to pass.

pARt 3

16

Fallon didn't sleep. His Cupid body didn't need it. Still, as he lay on the slab in the special room of the Cupid Center, he felt more relaxed than he'd ever felt in his life. Or his afterlife.

His mind drifted. Sometimes he closed his eyes, sometimes he kept them open. Other Cupids came to visit, but Fallon hardly noticed them. He felt good. There was warmth all around him. He thought he could lie there forever. For all he knew, he had.

Then, slowly but surely, his perceptions began to change. He started to take note of the people who visited him. Jada. Caleb. Even Louis, though he never looked happy about it. As time passed, Fallon began to pay attention to what they were saying to him.

Soon he felt restless. He still loved lying there, but he also felt an itch to move around. Still later that itch became an actual desire, and he twitched his arms and then his legs.

"Well, someone's coming around!"

The voice came from over Fallon's head. He tried to turn to get a look, but that kind of movement was currently beyond him.

"...who...?" he managed to say. His voice sounded very foreign to him, raspy and hoarse.

"Don't try to talk just yet," the stranger said. "Just rest. You are on the road to recovery."

Oh, Fallon thought. *That's a relief.*

He closed his eyes again, and his mind drifted some more.

Fallon paid attention again when he heard raised voices. Not surprisingly, Louis's voice was one of them.

"How I run this place is not open to debate, Caleb! I made a call, and it was the right one."

"Your call nearly cost Fallon his soul."

"Nearly," Louis said. "He's gonna make it."

"A few seconds more," Caleb said, "and he would have been lost."

"That's the risk that comes with the job."

"Did he know that," Caleb asked, "when you sent him to that school?"

"It was my call," Louis said. "Everyone survived, and the Suicide was destroyed. End of story."

"That's not what you said about Sandra," Caleb said softly, and there was a pause.

"That was different," Louis said.

"Was it?"

"You got no business bringing her up," Louis said. "You close your mouth, Caleb. You close it now, or..."

"Or what?"

There was another pause, and then Fallon heard footfalls walking away. He opened his eyes and saw Louis storming out of the room.

"I think you hurt his feelings," Fallon said.

Caleb spun around sharply and looked down at him. "Fallon! You're back with us."

"Yep," Fallon said, enjoying the joy on Caleb's face. His teacher had obviously been very concerned for him. "So," he asked, "what was that all about?"

"How much did you hear?" Caleb asked.

"Pretty much all of it," Fallon said, attempting to sit up. To his surprise, he succeeded.

"Easy, son, easy!" said a voice behind him, and firm hands took hold of his shoulders. "You're not going anywhere until I say."

Fallon looked behind him, and immediately recognized the old yet kind face he'd seen when he'd been brought in.

"I'm just sitting up," he said. "Who are you, anyway?"

"This is Alexander," Caleb said. "You might say he's our doctor."

"I'm a healer," Alexander said, easing his grip on Fallon's shoulders. "You're in my Healing Chamber. When one of you suffers a severe Suicide attack, I'm the one that brings you back."

"Oh," Fallon said. "Thanks."

"My pleasure," Alexander said. "You're not quite healed yet, so don't think of getting off this table."

"I'm a lot better than I was," Fallon said, and he stood up. The moment his bum left the slab, he nearly collapsed. Caleb caught him and eased him back down.

"I did warn you," Alexander said.

"The table"—Caleb rapped his knuckles on its surface—"channels Love directly into your body. Alexander directs it through you, healing you."

"But the process can't work if you aren't on the table," Alexander said. "So don't move."

"Gotcha," Fallon said. "I thought I just needed to eat some Love. That's what I did last time."

"Your last attack was considerably less severe," Caleb reminded him.

"Oh, been attacked before, have we?" Alexander said. "You'll have to learn to defend yourself better. Next time I might not be able to save you."

"I ran out of Love," Fallon explained. "Besides, if I'd known there was a Suicide in that school . . ."

"No excuse," Alexander said. "You should always be prepared to deal with Suicides."

"Even if I'm used as bait?" Fallon asked, turning to Caleb.

"Unfortunately, yes," Caleb said. He looked away, as if he were ashamed. "Louis has some ... unorthodox schemes for apprehending Suicides. That one at that school has eluded us for some time ... I'm sorry, Fallon. It should not have gone badly for you. Jada and Owen were sent to watch your back and intervene the moment the Suicide appeared."

"Well, they didn't do a very good job, did they?" Fallon said.

"They captured and destroyed the Suicide," Caleb pointed out.

"Maybe they did," Fallon conceded. "But they only caught one."

"There was another Suicide?" Caleb said, meeting his eyes once more.

"Worse," Fallon said. "The second one wasn't a dead person. It was my old friend, Susan Sides."

"That's not possible," Alexander said. "A person becomes a Suicide after death, never before."

"Well, it's true," Fallon told him. "She's the one that nearly finished me."

"Fallon," Caleb said, "what you are suggesting ... "

"Not suggesting," Fallon said. "Telling."

" ... is entirely without precedent," Caleb finished.

"Then I've got a first for you guys." Fallon said. "I was on the floor, and she stepped in me. Literally stepped in me! The second that happened, it was like she suddenly knew I was there. She could see me, too! And she knew she was destroying me." His voice sounded more defensive than he wanted, but he couldn't help it. If these two wouldn't believe his story, what chance was there that anyone else would?

"I must report this to Louis," Caleb said at last. "He'll want to hear what you have to say."

"I doubt that," Fallon said. "Say, Caleb? Who's Sandra?"

Caleb, who'd turned to walk out, stopped and hung his head.

"Sandra is Louis's daughter," Caleb said. "Please don't mention her to him; it is a very painful subject."

"How come?" Fallon asked, though he had a fairly good idea.

"She killed herself," Caleb said, then he turned and left the room.

It didn't take Caleb long to find Louis. The Cupid boss stormed into the Healing Chamber ten minutes later, glaring with visible impatience.

What a shock, Fallon thought as he sat himself up again.

"Caleb tells me you're making up stories about live Suicides again," Louis said. "Get it straight—there ain't no such thing, got it?"

Fallon groaned and gave the Cupid boss the dirtiest look he could muster. Then he slapped Louis hard in the face.

Louis, astonished, took a step back, eyes bulging. Caleb, standing behind him, was similarly shocked.

"Stop being stupid," Fallon said. "I'm not making up stories, I'm telling you what happened to me."

Louis recovered his composure and raised his hand, fingers ready.

"Don't you dare!" Alexander shouted. "This is my Healing Chamber, Louis, and he is my patient. You will not discipline one of my patients while they remain under my care. Are we clear?"

Louis looked at him for a long moment, then lowered his arm.

"Are you ready to listen now?" Fallon asked.

Louis shook with anger, ready to explode. He clenched and unclenched his fists and his eyes bored into Fallon like drills.

Fallon was sorely tempted to push his luck, take advantage of the situation, but he did not. This was serious business, with too much at stake. Besides, while Caleb had been looking for Louis, Fallon had thought about what he'd said about their Cupid boss. He understood Louis a little better now, saw where he was coming from and what was driving him.

But that didn't mean he had to take his crap.

Caleb stepped forward and gently laid a hand on Louis's shoulder. "Let him speak," he said. "I do not believe he is lying."

"You owe me that much," Fallon said.

Louis took a number of deep breaths and visibly calmed himself down. Fallon guessed he didn't do that very often.

"Okay, kid," he said at last. "Make it quick."

17

Fallon told Louis, Caleb, and Alexander his story in as much detail as he could. He did, however, leave out the part about his venture into the girls' shower room. It didn't really have any relevance to the proceedings. Plus, it was embarrassing.

Caleb and Alexander listened intently. Louis did his best, but still ended up interrupting several times. Each time he did, Caleb patted him on the shoulder and said, "Let him finish."

Once Fallon finished, he looked from Louis to Caleb to Alexander, trying to gauge their reactions. Alexander was wide-eyed with astonishment. Caleb wore a visage of dread. Louis just shook his head.

"There's got to be some other explanation," he said.

"There isn't," Caleb told him. "You heard what Fallon said."

"He hasn't been around that long," Louis said. "How's he supposed to know what he saw?"

"She had her foot in me!" Fallon snapped. "When I moved, she stepped in me again, on purpose! What's it gonna take to…"

"Fallon, calm down," Caleb said. "This is something none of us have ever experienced."

"Well, I have," Fallon said. "She's the reason I'm here. I wouldn't have been on that bridge, thinking of ending it, if she hadn't worked her mojo on me."

"You knew the girl?" Caleb said.

"Last year of my life, I couldn't get rid of her," Fallon said. "And right now she's sunk her teeth into someone else. If we don't move fast…"

"I'll get a team together, send them to the school," Louis said. "We'll check her out, see if your story's true."

"I'm on the team," Fallon said.

"No, you're not," Louis told him. "You're still in recovery. And you don't have enough experience with Suicides."

"I have experience with her," Fallon argued, gritting his teeth and closing his hands into fists. Couldn't Louis see this was personal? "Besides, my lack of experience wasn't an issue when you sent me to that school as bait."

"Hey! I don't remember you being promoted," Louis said. "What I say still goes. You're reassigned to another area just as soon as you're well."

"But I have to go back!" Fallon said.

"No, you don't," Louis said. "That's the last I wanna hear about it. You're already on thin ice with me, mister. Don't push it."

Fallon sighed as Caleb and Louis turned and headed for the door. He wanted to say more, but what was the use? He'd been damned lucky to get Louis to listen to any of his story. And had he really slapped him in the face? He smiled at the memory. He would pay for it, for certain, but that didn't stop it from being immensely satisfying.

"Please lie down," Alexander said, taking Fallon's shoulders and gently but firmly pushing him back onto the slab.

Fallon let him. There was no point in sitting up unless he planned to get up, and he wasn't ready to leave the Healing Chamber yet. He felt ready, but knew it was an illusion. If he left the slab, he would collapse once more.

He lay still for a while. He twiddled his thumbs. He rolled onto his side. He rolled back.

"How much longer do I have to stay here?" he asked at last. He felt wide awake, and the boredom was killing him. And the slab wasn't really all that comfy.

"At least a few more days," Alexander replied.

"You're kidding," Fallon said. He didn't think he could stand another hour, another minute, much less more than one day.

"I'm afraid not," the healer replied. "Now that you're

past the worst of it, I've reduced the amount of Love flowing through you."

"But won't I heal faster if I get more Love?" Fallon asked.

"Yes, you would," Alexander replied, "but there is a limit to how much Love I can withhold from the other Cupids."

Fallon frowned at that. "What do you mean?"

"Oh, I'm sorry," Alexander said. "How could you know? When a Cupid is brought in here to be healed, I must redirect Love away from the main flow. Sometimes, like in your case, I must redirect it all."

Fallon thought about that. "Are you telling me," he asked, "that while I was being healed, none of the other Cupids were getting any Love?"

"For the first week, yes," Alexander said. "Their Love cubes remained static, until…"

"The first week?" Fallon nearly leapt off the slab. "How long have I been here?"

"You should concentrate on your recovery," Alexander said, turning away. "I don't think that now is the best time to…"

"How long," Fallon repeated, "have I been here?"

"Almost a month," Alexander said.

"A month," Fallon repeated, and he lay back down again.

"Twenty-six days, to be precise," Alexander told him. "We've never had a Cupid in here that long. When I first looked at you, I feared you were too far gone. There have been others who were not as fortunate as yourself, Richard."

"Call me Fallon," he said, lying still and thinking about what he'd just been told. A month? That was a long time. Okay, not as bad as a year, but still …

He'd missed his talk with Trina! She was his best hope for helping her group of friends. And he kind of liked her. A sweet person with an unusual gift. Very cool. Not a popular girl, but to Fallon that just made her more interesting.

And he'd left her hanging. Not his fault, but she didn't know that. Fallon decided he would go back to the school, no matter what Louis said. He needed to talk to Trina again, let her know he was okay, and find out what was going on there.

What had happened during the time he'd been away? Was Ryan okay? Fallon sat up, very worried, as he remembered Susan's current "friend." Last he'd seen, Ryan had not looked at all well. Was he holding out? Or was he thinking of …

Fallon thumped the slab in frustration. He had to know! But until he was well, he was going to remain in the dark.

"Troubling thoughts?" Alexander asked him. "Try meditating. You'll feel better, and it will help to pass the time."

"Meditating?" Fallon said.

"Sit up, place your hands on your legs, close your eyes,"

Alexander said. "Clear your mind and concentrate on accepting the Love from its Source."

"Okay," Fallon said. "What is the Source?"

"God," Alexander said simply. "If you do this right, perhaps you will meet him."

"Really," Fallon said, raising a skeptical eyebrow.

"It has been known," Alexander replied.

Fallon didn't know if he believed him, even though he was sure Alexander wouldn't lie. He'd also never meditated before, or had any interest in spiritual things. However, he wasn't going anywhere.

Fallon closed his eyes and gave it a go. It was more difficult than he thought to clear his mind; thoughts came at him from all over the place. He supposed they always did that, but he hadn't noticed because he hadn't tried to stop them before.

"This is really hard," he said.

"The first time always is," Alexander said. "Keep at it, and don't let yourself get distracted by ... "

"Fallon, you're up!"

Fallon opened his eyes and saw Jada standing in the doorway. She looked happy and relieved, and Fallon liked to think both of those emotions were directed at him.

"When did you, you know, wake up?" she asked as she walked toward him.

"Not so long ago," he replied. "I'm not completely better yet, so feel free to shower me with sympathy."

Jada laughed at that, a wonderful sight to see. It almost

made him forget she'd been in on the plan to use him as bait.

Almost. But not quite.

"You can have all the sympathy you want," she said. "I'm just glad that ... you know."

"You mean, when you, Owen, and Louis set me up as a patsy, you're glad I wasn't completely and utterly destroyed."

"It wasn't like that!" Jada said, her voice pleading. "We were watching you the whole time. I honestly thought we'd get the Suicide before he could hurt you."

"Well, you didn't," Fallon said. Jada looked mortified, which was fine with Fallon. She ought to feel bad.

"Hey, at least I don't peek in on girls taking a shower," Jada said, crossing her arms over her chest and staring at him pointedly.

"You saw that?" It was Fallon's turn to look mortified. "I didn't know I was walking into the showers!"

"You didn't exactly hurry away when you found out," Jada replied.

Fallon opened his mouth to say something, but what could he say? Jada was right, after all.

"That's enough," Alexander said, stepping between them.

"Oh, sorry, is this bad for him?" Jada asked.

"No," Alexander replied. "It's just annoying."

"Look," said Fallon, "I've got to know what's going on

at the school. There's this girl there named Susan Sides. Has Louis told you about her?"

"He did, yeah," Jada said. "He sent Owen and me to check her out, and Owen touched her heart."

"And?" Fallon pressed.

Jada paused before responding. Fallon took that as a bad sign.

"She's not a Suicide," Jada said. "I'm sorry, Fallon. You were wrong."

18

Fallon had been told many times before that he'd been wrong. He doubted very strongly that this would be the last. However, as he sat on the medical slab staring at Jada, he knew this was one of the many times that he was definitely—without any possibility of doubt—right on the money.

"No I'm not wrong," he said. "Your buddy Owen messed up. Susan's a Suicide, Jada! C'mon, it's right there in her name."

"No, Fallon," Jada said. "Owen's dealt with more Suicides than most here. He would know..."

"But none of those Suicides were inside a living girl," Fallon pointed out.

"That's because there are none!"

"Until now."

"Fallon, let it go," Jada said. "What is this to you? What are you trying to prove? That you're better than the rest of us because you've discovered the first living Suicide?"

Fallon stared at her for a moment. "Is that what you really think of me?"

"No," she admitted, looking away. "That's what Owen thinks."

Fallon heaved himself off the slab. Instantly he felt groggy and weak, but he forced himself to stay upright.

"You tell that idiot," he said, stumbling toward her, "that I'm concerned for the kids in that school. If I'm right, they're in danger. The same way I was in danger when I was her friend."

"You..."

"Yes," Fallon said, standing right in front of her. "I knew her. And during that time I became very depressed. Suicidal, even. You remember when I told you I fell off a bridge? She's the reason I was there."

"Oh," Jada said. "But..."

"I wanted to die that night," Fallon said. "And right now Susan's after someone else, a boy named Ryan. I don't want fame and glory, Jada. I want Ryan to live."

"Okay," she said. "Okay, maybe you're right. But there's no way to prove it."

"Yes there is," Fallon said. "Check Ryan. Feel his heart, see what she did to him. And watch her. Watch how she acts. You'll see."

"Okay," Jada said. "I'll have to run it by Louis ... "

"No," Fallon said. "He'll be no help here. Just go check it out. You'll see I'm right."

"If Louis finds out, he'll kill me," Jada said at last. "You owe me one, Fallon."

"Just go," he said, and Jada turned and left.

The second she was gone, Fallon collapsed to the floor.

"I didn't think you'd last that long," Alexander said, helping him back to the slab.

"I'm surprised you didn't try to stop me," Fallon replied.

"I didn't want to interrupt," Alexander said. "You have a very strong soul, Fallon. For what it's worth, I believe your story."

"Thanks," Fallon said, sitting on the slab. "Look, do you think you could try and heal me faster? I've got to get back to that school myself."

"Patience," Alexander said. "There is nothing you can do right now that isn't already being done by others. Try to meditate again, and I will up your Love dose a tiny bit."

"You're the best," Fallon said, and he closed his eyes and tried to clear his mind once more.

He focused on receiving Love from the Source. He pictured the Love like a red laser beam, firing down from the sky straight into him. All other thoughts he brushed aside, keeping his mind on that laser.

Warmth and peace surrounded him. It felt good ... so good that he lost focus and thought about how awesome it was. It vanished in an instant, so Fallon concentrated and tried to bring it back. Then he realized he was concentrating on getting the feeling back, not on receiving Love.

He tried again. He felt frustrated, but he let that go. He was starting to understand how it worked now. He needed a clear channel open between himself and the Source. Thoughts garbled the signal. Fallon kept his mind clear and focused, focused...

The peace and warmth enveloped him again. This time he stayed with it, finding the calm center of himself. Fallon became aware of a presence, something alive in the energy around him. He was a part of it, a drop in its ocean. The entirety of the universe was open to him...

"Whoa," Fallon said, breaking the trance and freaking out. "That's intense."

"How far did you go?" Alexander asked, then he saw the look on Fallon's face. "Oh, I see. Well done."

"What?" Fallon asked.

"Well, you look very moved," Alexander said. "I have little doubt you'd be crying if our bodies had tear ducts."

"Probably," Fallon admitted.

"I doubt you'd be in such a state," Alexander went on, "unless you've had an encounter with the Source."

"I guess I did," Fallon said. "It was... well... "

"You don't have to explain," Alexander said. "I've been there, Fallon. All the old Cupids have."

"But not the young Cupids?" Fallon asked.

"The practice of connecting to the Source," Alexander explained, "is not taught to the new Cupids. It is not encouraged, either."

"Let me guess," Fallon said. "Louis thought it distracted people from their work."

"Got it in one," Alexander said. "There was a problem for a while with some Cupids neglecting their work in order to meditate. Every organization has its bad apples. Louis decided the best way to handle the situation was to punish all Cupids by forbidding meditation. I disagreed, told him there are plenty of times when a Cupid has nothing to do. At night, for example, when everyone in a zone is asleep. Or early in the morning. But Louis would have none of it."

"He really likes being a jerk, doesn't he?" Fallon said.

"He's … driven," Alexander replied. "He has his good qualities."

"Does he ever show them?"

Alexander laughed at that, but it was a sad laugh.

"I hope you'll get to see that side of him someday," he said. "I assure you it's there, but after what happened to Sandra … well, I'm sure you can understand."

Fallon nodded. He supposed he could.

Fallon went back to meditating, and hoped Louis would see him doing it. That would really make him mad! The thought made him smile. Yes, the guy had lost his daughter to the Suicides, but that didn't give him the right to ruin anyone else's life.

Fallon realized he was thinking, and brushed his thoughts aside. He concentrated on receiving Love from the Source …

The scream cut through his awareness like a freight train through a cat. The scream was his name, and Fallon immediately knew the voice.

"Trina!" he cried, and he leapt off the slab.

"Fallon, come back!" Alexander called after him as he sprinted from the room.

The Cupid Center spun around him. Fallon felt dizzy, weak, but he didn't let that stop him. He leaned against a large Love cube for a couple of seconds; he'd been rash to rush off like that, but he had to get to Trina. Something was very wrong, and she needed his help.

Fallon looked at the cube of Love. There was a lot there, and this was an emergency...

He grabbed two fistfuls and stuffed them into his mouth. He felt better, but not perfect. It would have to do.

The portals were close. Fallon chose one and ran toward it, concentrating on an image of the high school. He felt the familiar shifting of worlds, and then he was back on the school's front lawn.

There was an ambulance and a police car in the main parking lot. Not a good sign. Fallon didn't run toward them. Somehow he knew—perhaps on a psychic level—that he was needed elsewhere.

Inside the main lobby, two ambulance attendants were wheeling a gurney through a crowd of curious students. Fallon ran straight through the onlookers to see the victim—it was Ryan. His wrists were bandaged and soaked with blood.

Fallon kept going. There was nothing he could do for Ryan, and he had to find Trina.

"Fallon?"

He looked up and saw Jada and a couple other Cupids standing nearby. Fallon ran past them.

Outside the boys' bathroom, he saw Trina slumped against the wall. She was holding her hands over her chest as if she'd been punched.

"Trina?" Fallon said, arriving at her side.

"Fallon?" Her voice was a choked whisper. "Where have you been?"

"Sick," Fallon said. "Susan got me. I nearly ... I'm lucky I made it."

"Ryan tried to kill himself," she said.

"I know," he replied. "I saw. But don't worry about him. He's in good hands."

"I found him," Trina said. "Susan was waiting for him outside the bathroom. I sensed he was in trouble and ran in ... found him on the floor."

"Is that when you called for me?" Fallon asked.

"No, I called 911," she replied. "I didn't scream your name until Susan touched me, right here." As she spoke, she tapped her sternum.

Fallon felt rage boiling inside him. Having disposed of one victim, Susan had moved on to another.

"You'll be okay," Fallon assured her. "I'll protect you."

But he had no idea how he would do it.

19

Fallon and Trina went outside to talk in private as soon as the police finished their questioning. Classes had been cancelled for the afternoon and everyone was on their way home.

"You don't want to be with your friends?" Fallon asked her as they walked.

"I do," she replied, "but this is more important. I have a lot to tell you."

Fallon couldn't help but be amazed. Trina had just had a tremendous shock, and then she'd been preyed upon by the world's only living Suicide. Anyone else would want to take the rest of the day off, yet here was Trina, ready to work.

"How are you feeling?" he asked her.

"Like the world is pointless and I have no reason to live," she replied. "Your friend really did a number on me."

"She's not my friend," Fallon said, surprising himself with the bitterness in his voice.

"Sorry," Trina said. "I didn't mean … "

"No, it's okay," he said. "It's just, what she does to people … and my people don't think she's for real. They say there's never been a Suicide in a living body before. But she has to be."

"Oh, I believe it," Trina said. "I found out something about her that might explain things."

"You have?" Fallon exclaimed. "Tell me! What is it?"

He really should have predicted what came next. The electric shock struck him in the back of the neck, sending him flying through Trina on his way to the ground.

He rubbed his neck and rolled over to face Louis, who was walking out of the school toward him and Trina. Trina, momentarily confused, sensed Louis's presence and backed away with a gasp.

Louis ignored her.

"I've tried playing fair with you," he said as Fallon got back up. "You keep breaking rules, keep stealing other people's Love. And Alexander tells me you ran out on him."

"Come on, Louis," Fallon said. "Enough with the shock treatment, okay? Can't you just talk to me like … "

Louis fired again, knocking Fallon on his ass once more.

"Obviously not," Fallon muttered, rubbing his chest.

"Fallon!" Trina said, rushing to his location. "Are you okay? What's going on?"

"I'm fine," Fallon replied, even though he was not. "Louis, this is my psychic friend, Trina. Trina, this is my boss, Louis."

"The one you said was a complete jerk?" she said. "Oh, sorry…"

"You made a living person aware of our existence?" Louis said. "Didn't Caleb tell you…?"

"Look, Louis…"

"No, you look!" Louis snapped. "You're not being protected by your buddy Alexander anymore, so…"

"Fine." Fallon walked right up to his boss. "Shock me. Get it out of your system."

"Will you two stop it!" Trina snapped. "I've been through enough for one day! I don't need to be referee to a couple of ghosts."

"Little lady," Louis said, "this isn't any of your concern. You shouldn't even be aware of us. Best if you left here."

"He's right," Fallon said. "Louis might accidentally hit you, and I don't know what that might do to a living person. I don't want you to get hurt."

"I'm not leaving," Trina said. "You two are going to stop this, and you are going to listen to what I have to say."

"You had your chance," Louis said, and he blasted her. Trina screamed, flipped in the air, and landed on the pavement with a thump.

"Trina!" Fallon rushed to her side. He tried to touch her, but his fingers went straight through. He was desperate to help her, but he couldn't do a thing.

"You bastard!" he roared, rounding on Louis. His boss was ready for him; the blast hit him hard in the chest, hurling him backward.

"We're gonna … we're gonna settle things, you and me," Louis said. He walked toward him.

And faltered. It was just a misstep, but Fallon saw it.

"You're right about that," he said, forcing himself to stand. It hurt to do so—the multiple shocks had done a number on his body—but he did it anyway. "Let's do this." He braced himself for another shock, and was not disappointed. It hit him in the gut, throwing him backward once more.

Louis advanced, then stumbled. He regained his composure and resumed his march.

He stumbled again.

Fallon hurt all over, but he forced himself to his feet. He looked at Louis, who had stopped and bent over, panting.

"You're running out of juice," Fallon said. "Aren't you?"

The look on Louis's face told him he was right. His boss looked exhausted, confused, and suddenly very afraid.

Louis raised his arm and fired. Fallon ducked under the blast, then threw himself at Louis with all his strength.

"Oof!" Louis cried as Fallon slammed into him. They

fell through the nearest wall, back into the school, straight into an empty classroom.

Fallon straddled Louis, pinning his arms to the ground. He wasn't about to take any chances with him. Satisfied that his boss was helpless, Fallon rained blow after blow down upon Louis's face.

It felt good. He'd wanted to fight back against his tormentor ever since he'd met him. And after what he'd done to Trina...

Trina! Fallon leapt off of Louis and ran back through the wall. If she was dead...

She wasn't. She stirred when he approached, rubbing herself where Louis had struck her.

"I can't believe he did that to you," Fallon said. "I'm so sorry, Trina."

"Don't be," she replied. "That guy is one serious freak."

"Can you walk?" he asked.

"I think so." She turned toward the sound of his voice. "It hurts, but..."

She stopped. Her eyes went wide and her mouth fell open.

"What?" Fallon asked her. "What's wrong?"

"I... can see you," she said.

"Really?" he said. "Oh. Wow. Um, so... what do I look like?"

"Like you're half-here and half-not," she said. "And... is that a heart on your chest?"

"Yeah, I'm not crazy about that," Fallon said.

Suddenly, Trina's eyes widened again. "Look out!" she cried, a second too late.

The blast hit Fallon in the small of the back. It hurt, but it did not throw him forward—there wasn't much power behind it.

Fallon turned and stood. Louis stood behind him, looking exhausted and beaten. He fired off another shock, but it barely reached a meter beyond his fingertips before fizzling out.

"You're done," Fallon said. He strode forward and punched Louis hard in the face. His boss staggered backward, fell to his knees, tried to rise, failed. Fallon had him.

"Are you ready to listen now?" Fallon said, then chuckled. "It seems if I want you to shut up and pay attention, I have to ... "

Someone slammed into Fallon from the side. He fell sideways to the ground, another Cupid on top of him.

"Hey!" He turned to see his attacker. It was Owen, and his fist connected solidly with Fallon's jaw. Fallon tried to raise his arms to ward off any further blows, but suddenly he found his arms and legs pinned by more Cupids.

Owen punched him again and again and again. Fallon struggled hard, but he could not free himself. His vision was starting to blur, but he could make out two Cupids helping Louis to his feet.

"I knew there was something wrong with you," Owen said. "Never figured you'd break our biggest law, though."

"And what would that be?" Fallon asked.

"Assaulting the Cupid Leader," Owen told him. "You're in big trouble, mister."

"He was trying to protect me," Trina said, and the Cupids looked at her in surprise.

"Louis attacked her," Fallon said. "She can see and hear us, and was about to … "

"Shut up," Owen said, and he thumped Fallon again. "We're taking you back. You can answer to the angels."

"No," Louis said, his voice barely above a whisper. "Put him in Limbo."

"Limbo?" Owen asked, frowning. Fallon thought he looked conflicted, but it only lasted a moment.

"You heard the man!" Owen told the assembled Cupids. "Take him to Limbo."

Fallon had no idea what Limbo was, but from the way he was grabbed and hauled up by the other Cupids, he guessed it couldn't be a good thing. He tried to struggle, but all that got him was a punch in the gut.

"Don't get cute," Owen said.

He caught Trina's eye. She mouthed some words at him. Then the Cupids dragged him away.

20

Fallon emerged through the portal into the Cupid Center, his arms firmly held by his two minders. Owen walked along behind him, giving him a shove every few seconds for good measure.

Behind them, two Cupids carried Louis. It was dawning on Fallon that Louis had called for this team of enforcers during their little brawl. It was also dawning on him that he'd been galactically stupid, picking a fight with his boss. He'd acted on impulse—the man had attacked Trina, an innocent teenager.

Louis had also seemed very interested in not letting her speak.

But speak she had, silently. It had taken Fallon a few

moments to work out what she'd said, then to process it: *"She died and came back."*

Fallon wasn't sure what Trina meant by that, but it raised some intriguing possibilities. What if Susan had once been a normal girl who'd been attacked by a Suicide? Supposing she'd killed herself, only to be brought back in a hospital? Was it possible that she'd become a Suicide before her revival?

That raised more questions. Was she aware of what she was doing, on a conscious level? She'd recognized him when she'd stepped in and drained him. Had her awareness come about right then, or had she always known that she walked in two worlds?

Interesting questions, but right now Fallon had more immediate concerns.

"So what is Limbo, anyway?" he asked, turning to Owen.

"You'll find out," Owen replied, punctuating the thought with another shove. "Keep moving."

"You said I should answer to the angels," Fallon said, "before Louis pulled rank."

"Normally that's what would happen," Owen said. "But Louis says Limbo, so you get Limbo."

"I see," Fallon said. And he did. Suddenly he understood very clearly. Louis's attack had almost prevented him from learning what Trina had to say. And he didn't want Fallon pleading his case to the only beings whose authority was greater than his.

So Louis knew all about Susan Sides. And he wasn't going to do anything about it. And the only person who was any kind of threat to him was being sent off to Limbo.

"This place sucks," Fallon said.

"Shut up," Owen said, shoving him again.

They walked across the Cupid Center to the far side. During that walk, Fallon noticed how all the other Cupids were looking at him. Some stared in open contempt, others turned away and avoided eye contact. Some gave him smug looks, others had faces of pity.

One Cupid looked from Fallon to Louis and back again, then nodded and pumped his fist discreetly.

So they don't all hate me, Fallon thought with a smile. That's something.

When they got to their destination, Fallon recognized the spot; it was the area where he'd first entered the Cupid Center months ago, just after he'd died. There was a portal arch there, identical to the ones on the Center's far side. Fallon hadn't noticed it when he'd first come through, but its presence made sense.

They'd stopped next to Louis's huge Love cube; his two helpers brought him over and helped him feed. When he finished eating, Louis was able to stand without their aid.

"Let's do this thing," he said, and walked over to the portal. Fallon noted with no small amount of satisfaction that Louis still looked weak and beaten.

"Anything you wanna say to me, Richard Fallon?"

Louis said, activating the portal. Beyond it, all Fallon could see was white, empty nothingness.

"Yeah, I do," Fallon said. "Is it worth it?"

"Is what worth it?"

"Whatever the Suicides are giving you," Fallon said, "to keep Susan Sides a secret."

Louis laughed, but it was forced. "Makin' stuff up ain't gonna help you," he said. "Walt, Joe, put him in."

The Cupids holding Fallon yanked him forward, toward the portal. Fallon struggled fiercely—he was terrified. He had no idea what would happen to him; was Limbo anything like Hell? Was it, in fact, Hell? He could still see nothing in there but emptiness.

Fallon looked around desperately, hoping to see Caleb or Alexander or even Jada rushing to his rescue. Word had spread—they must've known what was about to happen.

However, there was no help in sight. There was a small crowd, though; his punishment had drawn a lot of interest.

Walt and Joe kept a firm grip on him, resisting his efforts to escape. They pulled him up to the portal, then Owen tied a cord around his waist. What, Fallon wondered, was that for?

"Listen to me," he said desperately. "I'm not making this up, I swear! Louis is putting you all in danger..."

"Shut up," Owen said, and booted Fallon hard in the rear. At the same moment, Walt and Joe let him go. Fallon fell forward into the portal, and a tingling sensation enveloped him ...

He was aware of having no body. He looked up, and saw his body hanging by the cord from the portal. He tried to move toward it but couldn't; Owen pulled the empty body up and out.

Nothing existed now except the portal's opening. Fallon could see the Cupid Center beyond, but found himself unable to move toward it. If anything, he seemed to be drifting away.

Louis walked into view and looked at him. Fallon looked back; there was nothing else to look at. He half-expected Louis to offer up a smug smile. After all, he'd won.

However, Louis didn't. Instead, he gave Fallon a serious look. Was that regret, Fallon wondered? Was it possible Louis still had a conscience somewhere in there?

The portal began to close. Fallon panicked, and struggled to move, but the portal did not get any closer. In seconds it was gone, and Fallon was alone in the nothing.

There was only whiteness, in every direction. In fact, the concept of direction was meaningless now.

So was motion. There was nowhere to move to. Fallon realized he was going to get very bored, very fast.

And then he might just go insane. Maybe that was the point of this place.

If he let that happen, Trina and everyone at that school were as good as dead. Nobody deserved that. He had to get out of there and stop Susan. Of course, that was easier thought than done.

Fallon wanted to close his eyes and block out the whiteness, but he wasn't seeing with eyes now. He had no body, and his soul couldn't stop perceiving what was—or wasn't—around it.

He had no body. That realization was freakiest of all. He was nothing now, lost in a universe of nothingness ...

No! As long as he could think, he existed. And if he existed, there was hope.

First, he had to find a way to stay sane. He would not let this place get to him. But what could he do to keep the emptiness at bay? Being here was even more boring than lying on the slab in the Healing Chamber ...

And what, he asked himself, had he done to fight the boredom there? He'd meditated. And he'd contacted the Source. If he could do that here, he had a chance.

Fallon tried to focus. It was hard at first, since he couldn't close his "eyes." Then again, there were no distractions. He found that if he concentrated on the nothing, his thoughts melted away into background noise.

In moments, he was one with the Source. Instantly his worries vanished, and peace wrapped around his soul. Fallon forgot all about why he was there, or the things that he had to do. All he wanted was to remain in this void with the Source.

Nothing else mattered.

PART 4

21

Fallon might have stayed lost in the Source forever. He was happy there. He felt safe. He wondered if he was in Heaven. He realized he didn't care. There was nowhere else Fallon wanted to be, and he couldn't imagine a heaven greater than where he was.

However, something compelled him back. Something nagged at him, a voice from within the Source. Fallon wanted to ignore it, but he could not. It was someone who had to be heard.

Ricky.

I hate that name, he thought.

Why?

My mom gave me that name. Before she left.

She loved you.

Not enough to stay.

That's not fair, Ricky.

I said I hate that name! Don't call me that. Call me Fallon.

Your father's surname.

Yeah, Fallon thought. I like it.

More than the name your mother gave you?

Why do you care?

Fallon found the conversation more than a little irritating. And personal. What happened to the peace he'd been enjoying up until now?

You can relax later, Ricky, the voice said. *Right now there are people who need you.*

There's nothing I can do, Fallon replied. They stuck me in here, and there's no way out.

There's always a way out, Ricky. You just have to ask.

Ask who? And stop calling me Ricky.

I like the name Ricky. I always thought it suited you.

Jesus! Who are you?

Not Jesus. And this is the wrong place for blasphemy, don't you think?

Whatever, Fallon thought. Just go away and leave me alone.

Is that really what you want?

Fallon thought about what he wanted. Memories came back, and he remembered Trina Porten, left alone in the world with Susan Sides. And he remembered Louis, and what he'd done to him.

He wanted revenge on Louis. He wanted to help Trina. He wanted to stop Susan.

That's a start, the voice said. *But what do you really want?*

Isn't that enough?

No, Ricky.

Stop calling me that!

Why?

Like I said, my mother called me that.

What did she do to you?

She left us, ran off with some jerk...

What do you want?

I want my mom back!

Fallon realized it was true. For all the anger he'd felt toward his mother since she'd left, he wanted her to be there for him.

"My dad told me she stopped loving us," Fallon said.

That was a lie, the voice told him, not unkindly. *I've always loved you.*

If he'd had a body, Fallon's eyes would have widened. He felt the presence around him—really felt it—and from that sensing came discovery.

"Mom?" He asked, but only for confirmation. It was her, he was sure of it.

Yes, Ricky, she said. *And I've one or two things to tell you...*

. . .

Fallon blinked. Then he realized he had eyes once more. He felt … heavy. He'd gotten used to being a spirit. Returning to his body was something of a shock.

He tried to get his bearings. He was lying on the floor of a small room—very small, it turned out. He could reach up and touch the ceiling with his hand. There was light; even the smallest of places on the other side were illuminated naturally.

Fallon looked right and left. There were bodies on either side of him, most likely the other prisoners of Limbo. There weren't many, Fallon was relieved to see. He wondered how long they'd been here.

There'd be time for speculation later. Right now, he had work to do. Fallon placed both palms on the ceiling, and concentrated.

The ceiling melted away, and the floor beneath him rose to fill the space. Fallon stood up, and found himself back in the Cupid Center, right next to the Limbo portal. It made sense to him; they wouldn't want to drag the empty bodies far.

Ahead of him were the rows of Love, starting with Louis's cube. Fallon smiled and walked forward, tore off a large chunk, and started eating.

Oh yeah. That would get his attention.

Fallon tore off a second chunk for good measure, then began the long trek across the Cupid Center. As he walked, the other Cupids turned and stared. It seemed like only yesterday those same faces had watched in pity as he'd been frog-marched to Limbo. Perhaps it had been yesterday. It didn't really matter.

He was about halfway across the Cupid Center when he saw Louis approaching from the other direction. He looked much healthier; clearly the Cupid boss had recovered from their last encounter and probably recharged his batteries.

Fallon smiled again. Time for round two.

"Who let you out?" Louis shouted, hands still at his sides. He's afraid, Fallon realized. Well, he should be.

"Hey, I'm talkin' to you!" Louis barked as the distance closed between them.

Fallon remained silent and didn't slow down. Louis stopped, trying to block Fallon's path.

"Who let you out?" he demanded, and his hands came up. When Fallon didn't answer, he fired.

Fallon raised a hand and blocked it. A shield of energy projected all around him, keeping the bolts at arm's length. All around him, jaws dropped. Louis's was one of them.

Fallon couldn't believe he hadn't been able to do this before. It seemed so obvious to him now. Like Louis's electric bolts, the energy came from his life force. Rather than draining his essence, however, the shield drew strength from the power of its attacker. The more Louis fired upon him, the more Fallon's shield sucked in the shock energy, and the weaker Louis became.

And Louis knew it. Fallon could see it in his eyes.

"Have you finished?" Fallon asked him. Louis didn't reply; he simply stared back, stunned. "Good."

Fallon continued on his way, not even sparing his former boss a backward glance. It was a calculated risk—he wouldn't put it past Louis to shoot him in the back—but he needed the other Cupids to see he was unafraid.

It hadn't even occurred to Fallon to hit Louis. He was filled with such goodwill after his time with the Source, his anger had been set aside. All that mattered was getting to his destination, and doing what had to be done.

Because the Source had confirmed his suspicion about Susan Sides. She had indeed killed herself and become a Suicide, only to be revived. He'd need help to stop her, and he knew just where to go to get it.

Fallon reached the portals, thought of his destination, and stepped through.

Fallon stood outside Guildwood Mills High School. It was lunchtime. Divine timing, Fallon thought as he walked across the main lobby.

There they were. Fallon saw Trina and her friends having lunch in their usual spot by the main doors. There were two notable absentees: Ryan and Susan.

Fallon knelt beside Trina and waited for her to sense his presence. She turned immediately to look at him, and mouthed his name. He smiled, then put a finger to his lips. No need to embarrass her in front of the others.

"We need to talk," Fallon told her. "Can you get away?"

Trina excused herself from the group and followed Fallon outside.

"What happened to you this time?" she asked when they were alone.

"Long story," Fallon replied. "I'm ... more than I was, Trina. Louis can't hurt me anymore."

"Well, he sure hurt me," she said. "He's not around, is he?"

"He'll be coming," Fallon said, "but I'm more concerned about Ryan and Susan."

"Ryan's taking some time off from school," Trina said. "He'll be at home. And Susan ... she didn't show up today! Do you think ...?"

"Yes, I do," Fallon replied. "She's with him."

22

The bus ride out to Ryan's place was too long for Fallon's liking, even though it only took twenty minutes. He was also feeling annoyed because he'd been unable to climb onto or off the bus without Trina's help. It only had the one step, but that was enough. He'd hoped that stair climbing would have come with the ability to shield himself, but no such luck.

Trina hadn't even asked if she should skip school to accompany him. To her, this was the right thing to do, and Fallon was deeply proud of her.

When they arrived in Ryan's neighborhood, Trina led Fallon from the bus stop to the nearest side street. "It's one of these," she said, pointing at a trio of houses in the cul-de-sac. "That one, I think."

"Are you sure?" Fallon asked her.

"I only came over the one time," she admitted. "And it was night. But I'm positive it's one of these three."

"Okay. I'll check them out," Fallon said, and he walked quickly over to the first house and vanished through the front door.

Two minutes later he reappeared.

"Not this one," he said, together with the unspoken prayer that he would never walk in on old people having sex ever again.

The next house was a lot more promising; Fallon entered into the living room and saw photos of Ryan on the wall. He searched the main level and found no one, but he heard voices when he reached the main stairs. Susan Sides. She was here, and she was with Ryan.

Fallon ran at the stairs, and was in up to his chest when he realized he still couldn't do it. He backed out of the stairs and concentrated on meshing his foot with the atoms of the first step, but it simply wouldn't work. He needed a person to take him up. He needed Trina.

"I need your help," he said as he came back out through the front door. "She's up there with him, and … "

" … you need me to get you up the stairs," she finished for him. "No problem, let me … oh. Spoke too soon. It's locked."

Fallon couldn't believe he hadn't thought of that. He tried to think of a way around the obstacle, and was about to suggest she break a window, when he saw her pressing the doorbell.

"Stop! Are you nuts?" he said. "Now she knows we're here."

"Now she knows someone's here," Trina corrected. "She doesn't know who. And if we're lucky, Ryan'll come answer the door to find out. Or she'll come, and I'll deal with her."

Once again, Fallon was impressed.

"You'd better do the talking," he said. "She'll sense me if I'm too near."

"Then get lost," Trina said. "I can handle Susan."

Wanting to stay as close as possible, Fallon ducked back inside the house and hid himself in the living room. He watched the stairs, expecting to see someone coming down at any moment. A minute passed and nothing happened, so Trina tried the bell again. Fallon moved into the main hallway to see if he could hear anything.

" ... don't need to see who it is," Susan was saying. "Who'd be coming to see you at one-forty? It's probably just some door-to-door loser."

"I still wanna check it out," Ryan said, his voice weak and with more than a trace of desperation.

"Oh, no, mister, you stay in bed," Susan said. "I have to take care of you."

Crap, Fallon thought as he darted back outside. "She's not letting him out of the room," he told Trina.

"I'll get his attention," Trina said. "I'll be back."

She hurried around the side of the house. Fallon walked back inside, wondering what Trina was up to, and saw her reappear in the backyard. As he watched through the kitchen window, she tossed a small pebble that struck one of the upstairs bedroom windows with an audible clonk.

"What was that?" Ryan asked.

"Stay in bed, I'll check," Susan said, but Fallon could hear the sound of rustling bedclothes.

"It's Trina," Ryan said.

"What does she want?" Susan said, and there was an edge to her voice.

She suspects something's up, Fallon thought.

"I'm gonna go let her in," Ryan said, and his footfalls left the bedroom.

"No! Tell her to go away," Susan said as her footfalls chased his. "You don't need her, you've got me!"

Now she sounds desperate, Fallon thought. He liked the thought of that. He moved in closer to the stairs and crouched down to get a view of the upstairs landing. He saw Ryan appear, but before the boy could descend the stairs, Susan grabbed him.

"Stop," she said, her hand on his chest. Ryan, who already looked like a miserable wreck, depressed further and slumped to the floor.

She's zapping him, Fallon realized, feeling equal parts anger and frustration. He was so close, yet not close enough.

"See? Look at you," Susan said. "You can't even stand. Let me take you back to bed. Trina will go away, and you can call her later."

Ryan breathed out heavily. He really didn't look like he could stand, let alone get down the stairs to let Trina in. When she knocked on the door, however, he tried. He pulled himself free from Susan's hands by sheer force of gravity, then slid the first few steps down on his bum.

"Ryan!" Susan called as she went after him. Ryan pulled himself down using the banister while Susan tried to snatch hold of his shirt.

They were close enough. Fallon stepped into the staircase, right into Ryan's body, and projected a force field of Love. It was similar to the shield he'd used to block Louis's power, but composed of Love instead of his life force. Susan stumbled into the shield, fell forward, and landed right on it, her face inches away from Fallon's own.

"You!" she snarled, and Fallon nearly laughed. He couldn't believe she'd actually snarled!

"Out of my way!" Susan shouted, hammering her small fists onto the shield.

"Not this time," Fallon said, and he expanded the shield outward by a meter. It happened so suddenly it threw Susan backward, up the stairs onto the landing.

Fallon smiled widely; it felt good to defend himself from—and fight back against—Susan's power. She stared down at him in surprise and shock. Now she knew she had a fight on her hands.

Behind him, Fallon heard the front-door lock unclick. Good for Ryan, he thought.

"Ryan!" Trina cried as she flung the door open. "Ryan, it's gonna be okay."

"Help me up the stairs, Trina," Fallon said. They could take care of Ryan later. Right now, Susan was the priority. He backed out of the stairs and let Trina pass him, then slid his hand into her heart.

In that instant, Fallon knew Trina's entire emotional landscape. She was pissed at Susan, and still felt a lingering sadness from when Susan had touched her. Trina was also very concerned for Ryan, and relieved that they'd got here when they did. Was she interested in Ryan? If so, Fallon had set them up. It was the least he could do.

But, first things first. Trina advanced up the stairs toward Susan, pulling Fallon along behind.

"Stay away from me," Susan said, scrambling back to her feet. She looked scared. Good, thought Fallon.

She turned and ran for the bathroom. Trina ran after her, but Susan slammed the door in her face and locked it.

"Don't worry about it," Fallon told Trina. "I can take it from here. You go take care of Ryan."

"Watch yourself," she said, then she headed back down the stairs.

Fallon, the floor now solid beneath him, stepped forward through the bathroom door. Susan cowered by the toilet; Fallon produced his shield and expanded it, flattening her against the wall.

"You're finished, Susan," he said.

"Ricky, please," she said. "What are you going to do to me?"

Fallon opened his mouth to tell her, but no words came out. He had no idea what to do with her. Projecting Love at her hadn't worked before, but that was really the only way to stop a Suicide. In order to destroy her, he would first have to get rid of her human body.

And that meant killing her.

He looked into her eyes and saw the fear there. He could do it; he could use the shield to crush her against the wall, but he was no killer. He wasn't capable of cold-blooded murder.

Susan looked back at him, and the fear was replaced with amusement.

"You can't do it, can you?" she said.

Fallon responded by pressing her harder. It had to be done—she had to be destroyed. If he didn't do it, how many like Ryan would be subjected to a slow, painful death? She wasn't going to stop, and he couldn't protect everyone from her.

He had to kill her. But he couldn't bring himself to do it.

"Fallon!" Trina called from downstairs. "Look out!"

He turned just in time to see Owen leap through the door toward him like a guided missile.

23

Fallon fell backward through Susan, Owen tackling him around the waist. They both passed through the bathroom wall and out the side of the house, plummeting to the ground. Fallon landed hard in the backyard, taking the brunt of the impact. Owen, cushioned by Fallon's body, rolled off him and climbed shakily to his feet.

"I'm starting to really dislike you," Owen said.

Fallon might have responded that the feeling was mutual, but before he could, he took Owen's foot in the guts.

"I don't know how you got out of Limbo," Owen added, "and I don't much care. You've crossed the line, big time."

Fallon was uncomfortably aware that, while he could

shield himself from energy attacks, physical punishment was another matter. He tried to get up, and made it as far as his hands and knees before Owen kicked him down again.

"Stop this!" Trina yelled, running from the side of the house and placing herself in front of Fallon. "Leave him alone."

Owen laughed and kicked through her, catching Fallon under the chin.

"Get lost, sweetie," Owen said. "There's nothing you can … hey! Cut that out!"

Fallon saw Trina waving both hands in and out of Owen's face. It couldn't hurt him at all, but it was obviously distracting. Fallon clambered back to his feet and was about to launch himself at Owen when someone slammed into him from behind. Two sets of hands grabbed his arms and pulled him to his feet. Fallon recognized them—Walt and Joe, the ones who'd thrown him into Limbo.

"What is this?" he asked.

"You just close your mouth," said Louis, emerging through the backyard hedge. Trina saw him, and had just enough time to register fear on her face before Louis blasted her in the chest.

"No!" Fallon shouted, struggling hard against his captors as Louis let Trina have it. She screamed but he didn't stop; the deadly bolts kept coming. Louis's face remained neutral, as if he were merely watching the news instead of instigating torture.

Fallon remembered his shield abilities and projected a field around Trina. Louis stopped his barrage, leaving Trina panting on the ground.

"Look what he's doing," Fallon said. "He's attacking a teenage girl! Don't any of you think that's wrong?"

"Boy needs some softening up," Louis said.

"Yes, sir!" Owen replied, walking over to Fallon with a look of pure evil pleasure. He threw a fist hard into Fallon's face; Fallon fell to one knee, his head reeling. Walt and Joe laughed and hauled him up again, and Owen threw another punch.

Fallon staggered against his captors but didn't pass out; it seemed his body wasn't able to. It also didn't seem inclined to break. His head absorbed the impacts, but it wasn't damaged much by them. The pain was as intense as Fallon expected, however. And if his body couldn't break or lose consciousness, Owen could take shots at him for as long as he wanted.

Source, Fallon thought, if you can help me, now would be a really good time...

"I think he gets the message," Louis said, then blasted Trina once more.

Fallon tried to project a shield but couldn't, and then a kick to his stomach made him forget everything else but his pain. He fell to his knees, and Owen reared back his leg for another punt.

"Stop!"

Fallon looked up and saw Jada rushing up to him. Louis pointed and fired a bolt at her, but then Caleb appeared and put himself in front of the discharge.

"Stop this," Caleb said as the shock waves coursed all over him. Louis stopped, but he did not lower his hand.

"Get out of here," Louis said. "This isn't your business."

"Louis..." Caleb said dangerously.

"That's an order!" Louis snapped.

"Stop this," Caleb said.

"I'm not warning you again," Louis said, his hand aimed at Caleb's chest.

"Neither will I," Caleb replied, and he charged. Louis fired, but the blast barely slowed the bigger man down. Caleb barreled into Louis, and the two hit the ground and rolled into the house.

"Owen, let Fallon go," Jada said.

"No!" Owen replied. "This is what he deserves, Jada. I caught him trying to kill a girl."

"Like Louis was doing?" Jada said, pointing down at Trina.

"She'd been helping him," Owen said simply.

Jada looked over at Fallon, and her face wrinkled. Fallon guessed that, even though he couldn't break, he obviously didn't look at all pretty.

"Owen, what are you doing?" she said. "I never knew you could be so..."

"Get lost, Jada," Owen said. "I'm not done."

Owen reared back his leg for another kick. Jada stood in front of him and said, "No. Don't do this."

Owen put his foot back down. Then he grabbed Jada by the shoulders and threw her to the side.

"Oh, you did not!" Jada said, climbing back up. "You did *not* just … "

"I said get lost!" Owen said, trying to shove her again.

Jada deflected him with her left hand and drove her right hand fingers-first into Owen's left eye. "Uh uh," she said, as he screamed and reeled backward. "One shot at me's all you get."

She followed up with a side kick so fast that Fallon barely saw her move. The blow knocked Owen off his feet, and he landed clutching his face. Jada gave him no time to recover; she walked over and grabbed one of his arms and twisted, then planted a foot on his back to keep him from moving.

"Not much fun being on the receiving end, is it?" she said. Owen swore at her, so Jada twisted his arm even harder.

"Havin' a little trouble with the lady, Owen?" Joe asked, and Walt snorted with laughter.

Great, Fallon thought. Not only are they brutal and evil, they're sexist, too.

"Should we help him out?" Walt asked.

"You boys think you can … " Jada said to them, then looked over their shoulders at something.

"Aw, don't fall for it," said Joe.

And that was the last thing he ever said. He and Walt suddenly went slack, all their muscles failing. Fallon fell from their grip; he crawled forward, then turned over to see what was going on.

Susan Sides stood behind them, her hands in Walt and Joe's backs. Her face was one of ecstasy, as if she were having the biggest orgasm of her life.

Walt and Joe slumped to the ground. Susan followed them down, her hands never leaving their hearts.

Fallon looked over at Jada and Owen, who stared at the sight with equal parts shock and horror. Fallon knew for certain that Jada had never really believed him about Susan. She did now, though. The evidence was staring her in the face.

"Let me up! Let me up!" Owen begged, and Fallon actually thought Owen might run to his friends' aid. Instead, the second Jada released him, he scrambled to his feet and ran off in the other direction. Jada shouted after him, then turned back to the situation.

"Fallon, what is she?" she asked, her voice on the edge of hysteria. Walt and Joe had lost their physical forms now, just like the Suicide that Fallon and Caleb had stopped. Their souls appeared, shining brightly—until Susan grabbed them. Their lights dimmed and greyed over, taking on the Suicide's astral aspect.

"She's a living Suicide, like I told you," Fallon said as

he crawled toward her. "Killed herself and became a Suicide. She was revived in a hospital."

"How do we stop her?" Jada cried, firing Love bolts that had no effect at all on Susan. "How do we stop her?"

Fallon had no idea. He knew they should run—they'd be next, otherwise—but then he saw Trina lying facedown in the dirt. If he ran, she'd be Susan's next victim.

Susan opened her eyes and her hands, and the two souls drifted aimlessly. At the same time, Caleb flew out through the wall of the house, blasted by one of Louis's bolts. He collapsed next to Trina, groaning. He did not look good.

Susan stood back up, looked at all of them, and smiled.

"This ... is ... awesome," she said.

Source, please get us out of this, Fallon thought, as Susan started toward them.

24

J ada, come here," Fallon said, crawling backward across the yard toward Trina and Caleb. "Do it now!" he added when she stared blankly at him.

Susan Sides was walking toward him—slowly, confidently. It was a bitter irony, Fallon thought, that she was finally showing confidence now.

"Shouldn't we run?" Jada asked as she arrived at his side.

"I need your help," Fallon said, taking her hand. "Project Love into me. I need your strength."

Jada nodded in understanding and linked her fingers with his.

Susan moved in, her hands outstretched.

Fallon projected his Love shield. Jada projected Love

into him, adding her power to his. The shield spread to encompass Caleb and Trina, and knocked Susan backward into the hedge five meters away.

Fallon smiled at that. It hurt to do so after Owen's punches, but he smiled anyway. Susan had just murdered two Cupids in cold blood; if he didn't try to smile, he would go insane.

"How did you figure out... this?" Jada said, waving at the shield with her free hand.

"The Source," Fallon replied. "I asked for help, and then I just knew what to do."

"Whoa," Jada said. "I never knew we could do stuff like this."

"There's a lot you haven't been told," Fallon said. "Isn't that right, Louis?"

Jada's head snapped around in time to see Louis emerging through the wall of Ryan's house. He looked haggard, beat... *the same way he looked after I kicked his ass,* Fallon thought.

"Will this shield protect us from him?" Jada asked.

"No, it won't," Fallon replied. "The shield that blocks him comes from a different source."

"Then shouldn't you..."

"He'd have shocked us already if he could have," Fallon said. "Beating Caleb wiped him out. Didn't it, Louis?"

"Not lookin' so hot yourself," Louis replied, raising an arm. "I got enough left for you."

"Do you?" Fallon asked. He was risking a lot; he didn't

think he could block both Louis and Susan in his current condition.

Luckily, he was right. Louis fired off a bolt so weak it barely got half a meter from his fingertips before petering out.

"Told you so," Fallon said. "Now talk. Why'd you come here? Why"—he turned to look at Susan, who was picking herself out of the hedge—"are you helping her?"

"I don't owe you an explanation," Louis replied. "What I do, I do, and that's the end of it. You got no business asking me anything."

"But I do."

Everyone turned again. Bud the Soul Reaper had emerged through the wall of the backyard shed, and he did not look happy. I've never actually seen him happy, Fallon thought, but this time he looks really honked off.

Fallon looked back at Louis. The man looked afraid, and seemed at a loss for what to do. He'd been caught; should he run, or throw himself at Bud's mercy?

Susan didn't hesitate. She ran.

Bud paid no attention to her. He approached the drifting souls of Walt and Joe and took them in his hands.

"I came here for these," he said, "but I will send someone for you, Louis. It's clear you're in up to your neck here. This does not look good for you, not at all."

The look on Louis's face changed, the fear giving way to misery.

"You don't understand," he said, but Bud was already fading away.

"What're you going to do about Susan?" Fallon called after him.

"Not my problem," Bud replied, just before he vanished.

"You don't understand!" Louis repeated, falling to his knees. "You guys just don't get it ... "

"It's about Sandra, isn't it?" Caleb asked, rolling onto his side so he could face Louis.

"His daughter?" Jada said, and Louis slowly nodded.

"They threatened her, didn't they?" Caleb said. "What have you done, Louis?"

Louis gave Caleb a dirty look, but had no words.

"Wait a minute," Jada said. "Five years ago when Owen and I got jumped by those Suicides ... is that what this is about?"

"I just know there's a story here," Fallon said.

"A group of Suicides surrounded Jada and Owen, and took Owen prisoner," Caleb said. "Which they'd never done before, at least not as long as I've been a Cupid."

"They told me to go get Louis," Jada added. "Told me to tell him if he didn't come, they would destroy Owen."

"So Louis went, and returned with Owen," Caleb said. "And you never did talk about it, did you?"

"They told me they'd hurt Sandra," Louis said. "You think you just got it bad?" He turned to Fallon. "You got no idea what a Suicide is capable of. They would've hurt her, my daughter, nonstop..."

"You made a deal with them," Fallon said, understanding. "The Suicides realized Susan could be the greatest ever—all their powers but still a living being, immune to the powers of a Cupid, as far as anyone knew. They didn't want Susan Sides discovered by the other Cupids, so they made a deal with you, didn't they? To leave your daughter alone if you left Susan alone?"

Louis nodded. "They told me they'll give Sandra back to me."

"And you believed them?" Caleb said.

"And this isn't the first time, is it?" Fallon asked. "Alexander told me how to connect to the Source. That's how I learned to make shields. You forbade the Cupids from meditating. Was that one of the Suicides' demands, too?"

Louis looked down, sighed, and nodded.

"Oh, Louis, you fool," Caleb said. "You poor, poor fool. They will never release her to you. And you've put lives—human and Cupid—in danger. How many like Fallon, Louis? How many like Walter and Joseph? How many have to die for your daughter?"

"As many as it takes," Louis answered simply.

"You don't mean that, old friend," Caleb said. "You can't."

"But I do," Louis said, looking up again. "I know what they'll do to her. And after all she went through in life..."

"Sandra chose to end her life," Caleb said, "and for

that, there are consequences. It is out of your hands, Louis. It always has been. Give it up now, before you make things worse."

"No," Louis said, and he shot to his feet. "No, there's still something I can do." And he turned and ran off through the house.

"Goodbye, old friend," Caleb said sadly.

Fallon wanted to say "good riddance," but he had enough tact to stay quiet. He looked away from Caleb and Jada and focused his attention on Trina. He touched a hand to her heart and felt her soul; she was still alive and appeared physically healthy, but Fallon felt damage that was more than just internal.

Source, he asked, what can I do to save her?

And then, he knew.

"Fallon," Caleb said, "what are you doing?"

Fallon didn't answer. He kept his hand inside Trina and poured in his life force. It was a risk that could cost him his existence—he had so very little life left to give—but it was the only thing that could heal the scars Louis had given her. Trina Porten didn't deserve to die.

Of course, he didn't either. But he would gladly sacrifice all that he was to give her the chance to keep going.

Fortunately, he didn't have to. Trina inhaled sharply and opened her eyes, then smiled weakly at the Cupids gathered around her.

"You're a trooper," Fallon said.

"Ryan," Trina said. "Is he ... ?"

"I'll check," Fallon said. He stood up, then promptly fell down.

"I'll go," Caleb said, and he started to rise to his feet.

"You're not going anywhere, Fallon," Jada said. "Neither are you, Caleb," she added, pushing the larger man gently but firmly back down. "You both look like hell. I'll go."

"Very well," Caleb said, amused, as she walked toward the house.

"Can she help him?" Trina asked, pushing herself up into a sitting position. "Susan got him pretty good."

"Only time, patience, and self-love can heal the depression a Suicide can cause," Caleb said. "We must find a way to keep Susan from him, so she can do him no further harm. And he must be watched, guarded. Depressed people attract Suicides like a moth to a flame..." He broke off, suddenly very worried.

"Oh no," Fallon said, catching on.

Trina would have asked, but just then Jada screamed. All three of them clambered to their feet in time to see her fall out of the house with three Suicides clinging to her.

25

Fallon and Caleb stepped in front of Trina and fired Love. Both were shaky on their feet, and neither's aim was perfect, but they did succeed in grabbing the Suicides' attention.

The three Suicides leapt from the fallen Jada and attacked. One came straight at the Cupids; Fallon and Caleb easily blasted it back. The other two darted to the side, then came at them from each direction. The two Cupids couldn't react fast enough; the Suicides latched onto them, and they fell.

Fallon tried to put up a fight, but he had no strength left. Looking to his right, he saw that Caleb was faring no better.

"What can I do?" Trina cried, but Fallon had no

answer for her. If help didn't arrive immediately, they were finished.

Fortunately, help came. A blast of Love knocked the Suicide off of Fallon, and a similar blast saved Caleb. The Suicides ran, unwilling to take their chances with this new threat.

Fallon struggled to raise his head and face his savior. Then he did a double take; it was Owen.

"You guys okay?" Owen asked, extending a hand to help him up.

"You've got nerve, asking me that," Fallon replied, ignoring the hand.

"Look, I was wrong, okay?" Owen said. "Louis said you were bad news, and I..."

"I know," Fallon said. "He saved you from the Suicides."

"So...are we cool?" Owen asked, his hand still extended.

Fallon considered, then gave Owen his hand. Owen helped him to stand, and then Fallon decked him full in the face.

"Now we're cool," Fallon replied, rubbing his knuckles.

"Thanks for coming back," Jada said, helping Owen back to his feet.

"Yeah, I kinda freaked out when...you know," Owen said. "They were my buds. And that girl who...I've never seen anything like that. Ever."

"No one ever has," Caleb said. "Is someone going to help me up?"

While Owen and Jada hurried to Caleb's aid, Fallon approached Trina. She looked worried and frightened, but she was standing again. Fallon realized he'd nearly given his life for her. In a second, he'd do it again. And the look she gave Fallon told him she'd do the same for him.

"Sorry I wasn't much help just now," she said.

"You're alive," Fallon said. "That's all I … whoa," he added as he fell over.

"Fallon!" Trina cried.

"I'm okay," Fallon said from his hands and knees. "Just a bit … woozy."

"You gave up part of your soul," Caleb told him. "And you were attacked by a Suicide. And then there was Owen's handiwork."

"I said I was sorry!" Owen said.

"We all need to get back to the Cupid Center to heal," Caleb announced.

"You guys go ahead," Fallon said. "Trina and I still have to help Ryan."

"You're in no condition to … "

"Ryan's not in great shape either," Fallon said. "If we don't help him now, he might not make it."

"You've lost too much life force," Caleb pointed out. "And more Suicides will come … "

"I've got plenty of Love left," Fallon told him. "And I can replenish my life force."

"How?" Jada wanted to know.

"Ask Alexander," Fallon said. "Once you get back. I'll join you shortly. Trina?"

"Yes?"

"I need a little help." He reached a hand up to her.

"Oh, right," she said, and leaned over so that Fallon could touch her heart.

When he did so, he suddenly felt a strong surge of emotion. She was feeling something more than simple interest in what she was looking at, and she was looking at him.

A flood of thoughts and feelings went through Fallon's heart and mind. Had he accidentally given her some Love when he'd been sharing his soul? Had the soul-sharing been enough to make this happen? He was happy, excited . . . and yet he was afraid. How could this possibly work out? He was intangible in her world, for crying out loud!

"Ryan," he said, breaking the moment.

"Right," Trina said, and she started toward the house. "He's probably where we left him." She was now feeling confusion and worry, and a tiny bit of heartache. Oh man, Fallon thought. What am I gonna do about this?

He was almost relieved when Trina walked through the front door and screamed. Her emotions changed instantly to shock and fear, and Fallon had to step past her to see why.

Ryan lay on the floor, surrounded by broken glass, his

left wrist bleeding. In his other hand he held a shard of glass with a jagged point smeared with blood.

The hallway mirror had been shattered—the source of the glass—and the phone sat on the floor beneath it. It didn't take a genius to see the two had come together violently, and the phone had won.

It took Fallon only a moment to absorb the scene, but Trina was already moving. She grabbed Ryan's bleeding wrist in one hand and squeezed, while her other hand took the glass shard from him.

"Find me something to dress the wound," she ordered. "Hurry!"

"There's jackets in here," Fallon said, looking in the hall closet. "A leather, a jean..."

"I need cloth!" Trina said. "Never mind, I got it." She threw off her jacket and peeled off her shirt, then wrapped it around Ryan's wrist.

"Ryan, can you hear me?" Trina shouted. "I need you to put pressure on your arm while I call 911. Can you do that?"

"G...go away..." Ryan muttered.

"Ryan, I'm trying to save you!"

"Leave...me alone..."

He's in it bad, Fallon thought, and immediately consulted the Source for help. The answer he got surprised him.

"Hold a piece of mirror in front of him," Fallon said.

"What?" Trina said. "Fallon, I've got to..."

"Do it!" Fallon said, kneeling beside Ryan. "Let him see his face."

Trina gave him a confused look, but she did as he asked. Ryan looked into the piece of mirror, saw his own face looking back at him...

...and Fallon fired Love into his heart. Ryan's eyes widened, and he grabbed his injured wrist with his good hand and squeezed tight.

"Help me," he said.

They helped him. While Ryan held his wound, Trina picked up the phone and called for an ambulance.

"You're really good in a crisis," Fallon said as she put the phone down.

"Thanks," said Trina, suddenly realizing she was almost topless.

"For what?" Ryan asked.

"I wasn't... never mind." Trina snatched up her jacket and put it on. "I need to make a tourniquet. Let me have your belt."

"I'll wait outside," Fallon said. He walked carefully through the door and sat on the front lawn.

Fallon meditated. It was tactically dangerous to do so out in the open, where a Suicide could attack him, but he needed the life energy from the Source. He tried to concentrate, but he kept thinking of how Trina had taken charge in saving Ryan's life. She kept surprising him with how capable she was. She'd whipped off her shirt without a hint of modesty, only concerned about doing what had to be done. People like that were rare indeed. And not bad looking, either…

Fallon shook his head to clear it. He needed to focus, and could not be distracted by how he was definitely *not* falling in love with Trina. She was a wonderful human being with a rare gift, and he respected her. That was all.

That was all!

Who do you think you're fooling?

Fallon wasn't sure if he'd thought that, or if the Source had spoken to him. Either way, it was true. He liked Trina. Wanted Trina. And, most likely, couldn't have Trina. He sighed, then tried to concentrate once more.

By the time the ambulance left, Fallon had more or less healed himself. He and Trina walked away from Ryan's house, and went the first two blocks in silence.

"Ryan'll be okay," Fallon said, breaking the silence. "I don't think he lost that much blood."

"No, he didn't," Trina agreed. "What was that you did to him? With the mirror?"

"I made him love himself," Fallon replied.

"Oh. Cool idea," Trina said.

"Just popped into my head."

"Neat."

They walked another block. Fallon wanted to say something—anything—but his brain wasn't playing along.

"So, you going to go back to school?" he asked her.

"No, I'll just head home," she said. "It's … been a strange day."

"Yeah, it sure has been."

"Besides ... " Trina folded her arms self-consciously over her chest. "I need another shirt."

"Right, of course." Fallon looked away. It had been all he could do not to stare at her when she'd taken it off to bind Ryan's wrist.

They walked a few more feet in silence.

"Do you have to get back?" she asked. "To your Cupid Center?"

"Yeah, I do," Fallon said, turning back to her. "I should check in with the others. Gotta form a strategy now that everyone knows about Susan."

"Oh. I guess, yeah."

"But I'll walk you home first," Fallon said.

"Oh, great!" Trina said, then caught herself. "I mean, thanks."

"Susan might still be in the area."

"Or that jerk of a boss you have."

"Oh, Louis," Fallon said. "I'd forgotten about him."

They walked another block, and then Trina pointed. "This is my street."

"Oh," Fallon said. "You're almost home, then."

"Yeah," Trina replied.

They walked a few more steps. I'm out of time, Fallon realized. It was now or never.

"Look, Trina ... "

She spun around to face him. "Yeah?"

"I ... need to say something. I mean, you and I ... "

"Uh huh?" she prompted.

Fallon fought his mind to find the right words and came up short. He wanted very much to say what was on his mind, but had no idea how to go about it.

Except to just say it.

"I want to be with you," he said.

"Really?"

"But I don't know how it could possibly work between us. Look," he went on, taking her hand in his, "I'm a Cupid, which means I'm dead! You're still alive … I'm just a ghost to you … "

"You're holding my hand," she said.

"I walk through walls!" Fallon said. "I can't even go up a staircase without help … "

"You're holding my hand," she repeated.

"I … what?" He looked down. And saw it was true.

He was holding her hand.

26

"Wow," Fallon said, looking at their joined hands. "That's ... wow. How do I feel?"

"Kinda tingly," Trina said. "Like I'm holding energy. It's nice."

She stared up into his eyes, and Fallon's mind cleared of questions. He leaned in toward her, and she closed her eyes and pursed her lips. Fallon brought his mouth down to hers ...

... and passed right through it. He retracted his head and tried again, but fared no better.

"It ... isn't working," Fallon told her.

"Oh," she said, her eyes popping open. "Um ... well."

"Look," Fallon said. "I ... ah ... "

"I know," Trina said, letting his hand go. "You've got

to get back. I should go too. I've got to come up with an excuse for skipping school before my parents come home."

"Right, yeah." Fallon watched as she walked up the driveway to her house. "I'll ... " Call you? " ... see you around?"

"I hope so," she said, flashing him a smile before disappearing inside her home.

Fallon waved and smiled back, but wished the moment hadn't been broken. He longed to talk to her about what was happening between them, but now obviously wasn't the time. He turned and summoned a portal, and returned to the Cupid Center.

Fallon went straight to Alexander's Healing Chamber. He suspected he would find Jada and Caleb there, and he was right. They sat on separate slabs, and both were deep in meditation. Owen was there, too; Fallon offered him a curt nod and a cold shoulder. Owen may have ended up on the right side, but that didn't mean Fallon was ready to like him.

"How are they doing?" he asked Alexander.

"They'll be fine," Alexander replied. "Jada's wounds were minimal, Caleb's more severe. There was little I could do for loss of life force before, but now ... "

"Where'd you learn that stuff?" Owen wanted to know. "And for that matter, how'd you escape from Limbo?"

"Yes, I'd like to know that as well," Alexander said. "When I heard Louis had sent you there, well, I thought you were done for."

"The Source," Fallon said. "That's the answer. I communed with the Source, and ... "

"The what?" Owen asked.

"I'll tell you later," Fallon said. "Right now we need to figure out what to do about Susan Sides. Caleb, Jada, can you hear me?"

Caleb and Jada continued to meditate, showing no sign that they had.

"That would be a no," Alexander said. "I know you won't like it, but we really should call Louis here to ... "

"Louis isn't coming back," Fallon said. He didn't know how he suddenly knew this, but he was certain of it. "Besides, he wouldn't help us even if he was here. Listen ... " And Fallon filled Alexander and Owen in on what he, Jada, and Caleb had learned.

"Whoa," Owen said. "Aw, man ... "

"I suspected something of that nature had taken place," Alexander said, "but I never dreamed Louis would take it that far. I pity him."

"I don't," Fallon said.

"Me neither," Owen added. "He used to be my hero, man! I'd have done anything for him after he rescued me."

"You did," Fallon reminded him.

"I said I was sorry."

"Don't be so quick to judge him," Alexander said. "If you'd been in his place, with someone you cared for threatened with torment ... "

" ... I wouldn't put others in danger," Fallon said. "He

did. I'll judge him all I want. I'm going to go eat some Love, then finish my own healing," he told them. "Come find me when these two wake up."

Fallon sat before his Love cube, meditating once more. It seemed the best way to pass the time. He'd really wanted to talk to someone about what had happened between him and Trina, but the only people he cared to talk to were in the Healing Chamber. Jada and Caleb were meditating, and Alexander … well, he could talk to Alexander, but not with Owen there.

The thought suddenly entered his head that he could talk to the Source. And it didn't take a genius to figure out where the thought had come from.

"Hello, Source," he said in his mind. "You'd think I'd be used to talking with you by now. This takes a lot of getting used to."

The thought that entered his head next told him that this was all right and hardly unexpected.

"Has this … what happened to me in Limbo, did it happen to anyone else?" The question surprised Fallon, even though he'd asked it. He'd been planning to talk about his holding hands with Trina. However, now that he'd asked, he realized he did in fact want to know the answer. Something had changed in him, and he hadn't taken any time to reflect on that until now.

It is rare, the Source told him, *but it has happened.*

"Where are the ones it happened to?" Fallon asked, and he learned that they had ascended. "Oh. Neat. Sorry," he added, feeling weird about using a word like "neat" with the Source. "Look, I … I wanted to ask about something that happened to me recently … " Suddenly he felt awkward. Was he really going to ask the Source of Love for advice on how to touch girls?

A feeling of peace came over him, and he sensed it was all right to ask the Source about anything.

"I … made physical contact with a girl," he said. "In the real world. I mean, alive. You know … how did that happen?"

An image of Caleb climbing stairs entered his mind's eye, followed by images of himself releasing a teen girl's heart as he arrived on the second floor of the high school.

"I don't understand," he said. And then he did. "You mean it's the same as adjusting to another level? It's all in my mind? Oh. But then … well, supposing I want to touch her again? On purpose, not by accident?"

Once again, he saw an image of Caleb climbing stairs. Caleb had learned to control his contact with differently phased matter through practice and mental discipline. Just as Fallon still had to learn to climb stairs on his own, so too did he have to learn to touch other out-of-phase objects, including Trina.

"Thanks," he said. "This is … well, um … is it okay to be having a relationship with Trina? I mean, this has got to be kind of unorthodox."

Fallon understood then that it was very rare for beings on one vibrational level to be aware of those on another, let alone have relationships with them. However, whenever there is awareness, a relationship often develops.

"Oh, cool," he said, and it was. His relationship with Trina had just received the Source's blessing. He felt happiness bordering on excitement and had to struggle to remain focused.

Enough about me, Fallon decided. Time for some important questions.

"What will happen to Louis?" he asked, and received an understanding that Louis's future was up to Louis. "Okay, how about Susan Sides? How do I deal with her?"

Fallon saw an image of Trina holding the piece of mirror in front of Ryan's face while he fired Love into his heart.

"I understand," Fallon said, and he brought himself out of his trance.

He walked back toward the Healing Chamber to find Caleb and Jada, only to see them coming toward him. Good timing, he thought, and gave silent thanks to the Source.

"I know how to stop Susan," he called to them.

"I'm glad to hear that," Caleb said. "The problem may be bigger than you know. I've just been consulting with the Source."

"Me too," Fallon said. "She didn't tell me anything about a problem." He didn't know why he referred to the Source as she; it just felt right.

"You have to ask the right questions," Caleb said. "I

asked what your friend Susan has the potential to become, now that she is aware of what she is."

"And?" Fallon asked.

"She has the potential," Caleb said, "to become a monster."

Fallon nodded silently. He'd feared Caleb would say something like that.

"She can hurt us bad," Owen said, filling the silence. "I never thought I'd see the day."

"There's more," Caleb said. "A Suicide draws power from the people they sicken. Susan can destroy a Cupid with only a few moments' contact. To the living, she may be an even greater danger."

"You mean … she can kill people with a touch?" Fallon asked.

"I don't believe she can kill," Caleb said. "But she might be able to inflict severe depression on the living without physical contact."

The gravity of that statement was lost on no one.

"No wonder the Suicides wanted Louis to look the other way," Fallon said.

"We gotta take her down," Owen said. "Hey, Fallon, that shield thing you were doing before I …"

" … beat me to a pulp?"

"Yeah," Owen said, looking sheepish. "Look, uh, you could do that thing again, right? Mush her against a wall?"

"That would kill her," Fallon told him.

"So?" said Owen.

"That's not what we do," Fallon said. "We're Cupids. We bring love, not death."

"You mentioned a plan?" Caleb said, cutting Owen's next remark off.

"We get her to love herself," Fallon said. "It worked on Ryan, the boy Trina and I were helping. We get Susan to see herself in a mirror, I fire Love into her heart, and her Suicide aspect will be reversed."

"You sure about that?" Jada asked.

"It came from the Source," Fallon told her.

"Then our task is clear," Caleb said. "Let's go."

27

Fallon, Caleb, Jada, and Owen emerged from the portal and stood in front of Susan Sides's house. According to the Source, it was where Susan was. Fallon had been skeptical—he remembered Susan ranting to him about how "my demon mother won't let me miss a day of school, even if I'm sick!"—but he trusted the Source's accuracy.

"Let me go first," Fallon said. "You guys can back me up."

"We go in together," Caleb said firmly.

"I can shield myself against her," Fallon pointed out.

"So can I, remember?" Jada added.

"I can't," said Owen.

"Nor I," Caleb said. "And we haven't time to learn. If we split up, we'll be in more danger. We go in together."

"Fine, but stay close to Jada and me," Fallon said.

They walked two at a time through the front door, Fallon and Caleb first. Bad memories came back to Fallon straight away—all the times he'd come to this place during the last year of his life. The invitations had always been under the guise of something fun, like renting a video. When he arrived, however, she'd always say, "Mind if we just talk?" And there would go four hours of his life, sometimes six, as she dished on her latest emotional crisis. He remembered the sensation of his life draining away, and now he knew she'd literally been doing exactly that.

"Fallon?" Caleb said gently, bringing him back to the present. "Those memories won't help you."

"I know," Fallon replied. "But I can't stop them."

"Focus on the here and now," Caleb said. "And what we have to do."

"Right," Fallon said. "She's probably in her room. This way."

For the first time, Fallon was grateful that Susan lived in a bungalow. Her room was at the end of a hallway that branched off from the living room and kitchen. He tried to stay focused in the present as he walked toward her room, but memories kept jarring their way back in. The bedroom door was closed; Fallon wasn't sure he could take seeing that place again.

"Do you want to wait out here?" Caleb asked.

"Yes, I do," Fallon said, "but I'm going in with you anyway. I have to do this."

Caleb nodded, and they both walked through the door.

Susan wasn't there. Fallon didn't know if he felt relieved or disappointed. The room was exactly the way he remembered it; messy but functional, with no trace of personality. She had a desk, covered in schoolbooks, next to her bed, which was unmade. The hamper in the corner overflowed with clothes, and the closet was packed full of all kinds of odds and ends from her seventeen years. A dim bulb cast just enough illumination to give the room its full effect.

"I feel despondent just looking at this," Caleb said.

"She's not in here," Fallon said. "Let's try … "

"Hey! Over here!"

Fallon and Caleb hurried through the door and went into the room across the hallway. Owen and Jada were inside, looking at a body on the bed.

"It's her mother," Fallon said, looking her over as best he could. She looked dead, even though Fallon could see no mark on her body. Her face bore a look of utter hopelessness, and the tears on her face were still wet.

She managed a blink. Not dead then, Fallon realized, just too depressed to move.

"Susan knows how powerful she is," Caleb said. "And she is still here. She must be."

"One of the other bedrooms?" Jada suggested.

"Her brother," Fallon said, and he ran into the room next to Susan's. This bedroom was much tidier and more cheerful. And, Fallon was relieved to note, there was no body. Of course, Fallon realized, Susan's brother was still at school. Then where...?

"Never do that again," Caleb said as he entered. "We stay together."

"Right, sorry," Fallon said. "I had to make sure..."

"We've lost enough people."

"Okay, I get it," Fallon said. "I'll check with the Source, see where Susan is..."

He had a vision of Susan's basement. She was sitting on the floor, her hands outstretched into darkness... no, not darkness. Suicides. She was surrounded by dozens of Suicides!

Her eyes flashed open. She smiled. She raised her hands over her head, and the Suicides flew up through the ceiling.

"Incoming!" Fallon shouted as the room suddenly filled with dark entities. He heard two screams from the other room; Jada and Owen were in trouble.

And so was he. Fallon blasted two Suicides back, then threw up his shield. He turned to Caleb and expanded the shield outward, protecting his friend from the attack. He hoped Jada had the presence of mind to do the same.

The Suicides didn't flee from the two Cupids. Rather, they hammered on the shield with gusto. It held, but Fallon didn't think it could take much more. He was reluctant to shoot Love at them, though—he needed it all for the shield.

Caleb was not so reluctant; he fired near constant streams of pink. For every Suicide he knocked back, however, another moved in to take its place.

"I've never seen so many in one place," he told Fallon. "Suicides are loners by nature. Susan must have rallied them."

"Let's get out of here," Fallon suggested. "Make a portal and ..."

"No!" Caleb shouted, startling Fallon. "We must defeat them. It is our duty."

"There's too many!" Fallon protested.

"Then help me reduce their numbers!" Caleb replied.

I hope you know what you're doing, Fallon thought, and he dropped the shield and started blasting. As he expected, the Suicides swarmed in. Fallon fought furiously, panic rising inside him. This was crazy, and Caleb was crazy, and they had to escape ...

And then Fallon destroyed a Suicide and it was not replaced by another. Their numbers thinned, and many chose to flee.

"We are stronger," Caleb said as he blasted the last of them. "We are always stronger. Let's help the others."

They ran across the hall into the master bedroom to find another thick fog of Suicides beating on a shield encompassing Jada and Owen. Jada looked beat; Owen was blasting with one hand and trying to help her up with the other.

"Little help?" he said.

Fallon and Caleb entered the fray, and the Suicides found themselves caught between the four Cupids. A few chose to fight, and were quickly destroyed. Most fled through the walls and ceiling.

"This is more like it!" Owen said, and he charged out into the hall after two of the dark spirits.

"Owen!" Caleb shouted, running after him. "Does no one ever listen?"

Fallon helped Jada to her feet, and they were passing through the wall into the hallway when Owen screamed. They ran to the living room and saw Susan Sides, both arms buried in Owen's chest while he screamed hysterically.

Caleb slammed hard into Owen's side, jarring him free. Before he could retreat, however, Susan caught him in the same deadly grip. Fallon and Jada rushed toward him, but Caleb waved them back.

"Save Owen," he groaned, already slumping in Susan's arms.

"No!" Fallon shouted, grabbing his hand and pulling. "Jada, help me!"

"Get Owen out…" Caleb said, and then he fell apart.

Fallon stared in horror at the sight, and at the bliss-ful look on Susan's face. Her legs became jelly and she fell to her knees even as she cried out. Then she giggled, her world well and truly rocked.

"That was awesome!" she said, opening her eyes. "Bet you will be, too."

"Fallon!" Jada cried. He ignored her.

Instead, he threw up his shield and pushed forward, knocking Susan back into the kitchen. He pressed her up against the back door and gave it all he had. Susan pushed back with her hands, which took on a dark glow. Fallon felt himself becoming depressed—good God, he thought, she can do it at a distance now? He ignored the damage it was doing to him and kept pressing. One way or another...

"Fallon! I need your help!"

Jada's voice called him back. Reluctantly, he had to admit he would lose this fight—his Love was nearly drained from the earlier fight with the Suicides, while Susan's power was fresh. Plus, Jada probably did need his help. He lowered the shield and stepped back, and Susan recovered.

Then Fallon flung his shield out like a fist, swatting her against the door. She cried out and fell, and Fallon left the kitchen quickly.

Jada had a portal open and was pulling Owen in by his legs. Fallon grabbed Owen's shoulders, and together they hauled him through the portal.

28

Fallon and Jada sat by the wall in the Healing Chamber, watching as Alexander tended to Owen. When Fallon had told the healer what had happened to Caleb, Alexander had nodded, once. At first Fallon thought he was being cold, but it occurred to him, as he sat with Jada, that the older spirit was just putting on a brave front. Everyone grieves differently, he thought, and wondered how his father and sister had grieved for him.

Maybe it was time for a visit...

The thought made him even more miserable. Caleb had been the one to tell him to stay away from family, for his own sake as much as theirs. Always looking out for everybody, Caleb was.

And, Fallon realized suddenly, Caleb had been the best

contender to take over Louis's job as leader of the Cupids. Who could possibly fill that role now?

"Is he a Suicide?" Jada asked suddenly.

"You mean Caleb?" Fallon asked. "I don't know." And he didn't want to. Susan's power could drain the life from a soul, leave it so negative that a Suicide was all it could become. But Caleb... he was stronger than most, wasn't he? But what alternative was there?

"Maybe he's, y'know... gone on to the next stage," Jada said.

"The next stage?"

"Paid his karmic debt," she said. "Gone to Heaven."

"Is that place even real?" Fallon asked.

"Supposed to be," Jada said. "At least, that's what Caleb told me."

They sat in silence for a while, until Fallon could take it no longer.

"I need some Love," he said, and stood up and left the Healing Chamber. He walked back to his cube, which was now depressingly small. He hadn't been out doing the job, and his cube reflected that. Fallon sighed and ate what little Love he had left, then sat down to meditate.

While in his trance, it occurred to him to ask the Source about Caleb. He dismissed the thought at once, and begged the Source not to tell him. If the news was bad, he really didn't want to know. Instead, he asked what Susan was currently up to.

Images and emotions went through his mind quickly.

Susan was really mad at him for hurting her during their last confrontation, and for revenge, she'd visited his family. Cold dread filled Fallon, but then he understood that Susan had failed to hurt his father and sister. His father hadn't even opened the door—he'd yelled at her through the living room window to go away or he'd call the cops. "It's your fault my son is dead, you little freak!" he'd said, surprising Fallon. Whenever Fallon had talked to his father about Susan, his father had said it was his duty to be her friend. "If you're all she has, take that responsibility seriously!" *It took my death to wake him up*, Fallon thought. Too little, too late.

Susan had left, angry and humiliated. She'd run into a group of teenage girls—the same ones, Fallon realized, who had mocked Trina in the changing room. Susan threw up her hands and blasted them with darkness, and the girls fell over. Susan left them there unable to move, barely able to breathe.

Onward she walked. A few Suicides joined her, circling around her like excited puppies. The people across the street from her slowed down; those on the same side collapsed as she passed them. Cars went out of control as their drivers suddenly lost the will to live.

And the Suicides fed.

Susan kept walking, and Fallon recognized the street she turned on to. She's going to Trina's house, he realized. He wanted to leap into action right then.

When Trina entered his focus, however, something happened. Suddenly he found himself looking through her eyes—he knew they were her eyes—and seeing what she was doing. She was sitting at a table in a fast-food restaurant with two of her friends from school, Cynthia and Lucy. He didn't remember their names; he simply *knew* their names, as if he were taking them directly from Trina's memory.

What, he asked the Source, is happening? And then he understood. When he'd given Trina part of his soul, he'd linked himself to her in a way he'd never expected.

"Trina?" Cynthia asked. "Are you okay?"

"I ... I'm not sure," she replied.

"Maybe her Rib'N'Cheese didn't agree with her," Lucy suggested.

"C'mon, let's get you home," Cynthia suggested, and they got up from the table...

"No!" Fallon screamed, and he was up and running before he realized he'd left the trance. He grabbed Love from cubes as he passed them—no time for niceties now, this was an emergency. If Susan was still there when Trina and her friends got to her house, he would lose her.

Fallon was almost to the portals when Jada came running toward him. There was something different about her, but Fallon didn't have time to reflect on it.

"Fallon, where are you going?" she asked as she caught up with him.

"Trina's house," Fallon said. "Susan's there. And she's got company. Lots of Suicides."

"And you're going to take them all on by yourself?"

Jada asked. "Is that why you're stealing from all the Love cubes?"

Fallon wondered how she knew about that, then decided he didn't care.

"Yeah, I am," he said. "Sue me. I have lives to …"

He didn't finish, because a shock hit him on the right shoulder. It was very mild and didn't hurt much, but it was enough of a surprise to stop him in his tracks.

"Did you …?"

"Yes," she said. "While you were off doing your own thing, an angel came to visit, and she appointed me the new leader of the Cupids."

"Really?" Fallon said. "That's great, Jada, and I'd love to talk some more about it, but I've got to go and …"

"Stop," she told him. "As leader, I decide who goes on what mission …"

"Jada, Susan is going to …"

" … and I say you are not going alone," Jada said. "We're not going to lose any more Cupids."

Jada turned and raised her hands, and Fallon heard a sound like an intercom coming on.

"Attention all Cupids, we have an emergency!" she said, and her voice broadcast across the entire Cupid Center. "I need every available Cupid to report to the portals for immediate deployment. This is a Suicide emergency! Eat your Love and let's go go go!"

Fallon watched, amazed, as Cupids rushed forth, stuffing Love into their mouths as they came. Jada saw him watching, and smiled.

"Louis only did this once," she told him. "I've always wanted to."

Fallon nodded, speechless. Jada was the Cupid leader; that in and of itself was a lot to take in. The fact that she was organizing a Cupid strike force to back him up, however, was blowing his mind.

"Listen up!" Jada called to the first Cupids to reach them. "We'll be facing a swarm of Suicides and a girl who is a Suicide in living form. Avoid the girl! She's too dangerous. Leave her to Fallon and myself.

"You." She pointed at a male Cupid. "Stay here and tell the others exactly what I told you, then send them in after us. The rest of you, you're my first wave. Let's go!"

Jada turned and strode purposefully toward the portals, and the Cupids followed.

"Fallon, if you would do the honors," she said, indicating the nearest portal arch.

"Right," Fallon said, and set the portal to open right in front of Trina's house. He and Jada went through first, just in time to meet Susan coming up the driveway. The street behind her was almost completely blacked out by her Suicide army.

"Hah!" Susan shouted. "Boy, did you two pick a bad time to ..."

Her jaw dropped as the army of Cupids arrived and formed ranks in front of the house. Then she trembled visibly.

"G ... get them!" she cried, and the Suicides surged forward.

"Shield!" Jada shouted, and she and Fallon projected a solid Love wall that knocked all the dark ones—Susan included—backward.

"Now charge!" Jada cried, and the Cupids marched forward and fired their Love. A dozen Suicides fell immediately, and several more dropped in the moments that followed. *Suicides have no projectile weaponry*, Fallon realized. *They have to get up close to do damage, and we aren't going to let them!*

Susan straightened up and looked at her army in horrified disbelief. Fallon had to smile. This is what losing looks like, he thought at her.

Then Susan saw something beyond her dark army that grabbed her attention. She turned and ran off down the street, leaving her army to fend for itself.

"She's running away!" Jada said.

"I don't think so," Fallon replied, looking through the fog of Love and darkness to see what Susan was after.

It was Trina, Cynthia, and Lucy, returning from the restaurant at the worst time possible. He'd hoped they would finish Susan off before the girls got back, but it was too late for that now.

Trina froze, then blocked her two friends. She could see the war going on, but all they could see was Susan running toward them.

Fallon ran, forgetting his shield and charging through the battle.

"Fallon! Come back!" Jada called.

Fallon ignored her and kept running, blasting aside any Suicide that got in his way. Susan had a head start, and could reduce all three teens to a near-lifeless state in seconds. He ran faster and prayed he'd be in time.

29

R un!" Trina told her friends. "Turn around, get out of here, go!"

Though he was still three house-lengths away, Fallon heard her voice as clearly as if she'd spoken beside him. Sadly, her friends saw no threat in Susan, who raised her hands as she closed the distance. Fallon felt waves of depression—Trina's, not his—as Susan's power reached out and engulfed them.

Our link is a little too strong, Fallon thought. Then it hit him that the soul link might work both ways. He focused his Love reserves into his soul and thought, *shield*.

Trina's hands went out, and suddenly she was projecting a shield of Love in front of her. Susan walked straight into it and rebounded onto her butt. She looked up at

Trina with shock and outrage—Fallon could see it clearly in his mind. He also felt Trina's puzzlement as she looked at her hands in wonder. Then she looked up at him, and their eyes met. Wow, Fallon thought, as he and Trina shared a moment of perfect bliss. There was no other on Heaven or Earth for either of them.

"Trina?" asked Cynthia. "Are you having one of your moments?"

"And what happened to Susan?" asked Lucy. "What's going..."

Susan threw both hands forward and soaked the three teens in misery. Trina got the shield back up again, but not before absorbing enough sadness to drive her to her knees. Her two friends collapsed, barely able to breathe. The only reason Trina wasn't on the pavement with them, Fallon knew, was that her soul was mixed with his. The assault had knocked the wind out of his sails, too, but he managed to stay upright and moving.

Trina was weakening. No problem, Fallon thought, projecting a shield of his own. It knocked Susan flat on her face, and Fallon walked right up to her and kept projecting, pinning her down.

"I need..." he began.

"...a mirror!" Trina finished, and she started going through her friends' purses.

Wow, Fallon thought, *now we're finishing each others' sentences...*

A Suicide broadsided him, knocking him over and fill-

218

ing his soul with despair. Fallon dropped his shield but raised another, then he pushed the Suicide away so he could blast it.

Susan got back up. Before Fallon could deal with her she stepped in him, and the depression soaked him.

Trina, back on her feet and with a mirror in hand, slammed her shoulder into Susan and knocked her out of Fallon. Susan recovered quickly and grabbed Trina by the wrist, and Fallon could feel the life pouring out of her. He got back to his knees but she stepped in him again, and Fallon knew it was over.

Source, he thought, *help...*

An electric blast hit Susan in the back, and Trina broke free. Fallon saw Jada running toward them and smiled weakly. Trina opened the compact and held the mirror in front of Susan's face, and Fallon thrust his hand into her heart and fired.

Susan's eyes went wide. Then she screamed. The crushing flow of sadness stopped, and Trina and Fallon collapsed at her feet. Susan looked down at them, horrified.

"What ... who ... what am ... " she said. Then she crumpled into a ball and cried.

"Yeah, you're darn right you feel bad," Jada said as she arrived. "And you, Fallon, need to learn to listen to orders. I said I'm not losing anyone else."

"H ... help them ... " Fallon said weakly, waving a hand at the three teenagers. " ... need Love ... "

"They'll get it," Jada said. "Trina, right? Can you still hold that thing?"

She nodded, and held the compact up to her face. Jada fired Love into her, and Trina sat up and smiled.

"That was groovy," she said.

"Come on, let's do your friends," Jada said.

Moments later, Cynthia and Lucy were full of Love and recovering. Fallon envied them—he couldn't get his healing dose until he got back to the Cupid Center.

"Trina," Lucy asked, "what just happened?"

"What did Susan do to us?" asked Cynthia. "Hey, what's wrong with her?"

"I'll tell you all about it," Trina said, "but first I have to help my friend." She moved next to Fallon, who smiled up at her.

"Hey, babe," he said.

Trina smiled back, and held the mirror in front of his face. Then she reached into his heart and gave him a shot of his own Love.

"Whoa …" Fallon said as self-love replaced the crippling despair. Trina put down the compact, but she let her hand linger in Fallon's heart a moment longer.

"I figured I owed you one," she said, and smiled that perfect smile of hers.

"Not as much as I owe you," Fallon said, and he sat up and kissed her.

The assembled Cupids gasped. So did Trina's friends.

"Look!" said Lucy. "Can you see … a sort of ghostlike thing?"

"She's kissing a ghost," Cynthia replied. "And he's pretty good."

"How is that possible?" a Cupid asked.

"I guess anything's possible," Jada replied, smiling down at them. "Hey, get a room, you two!"

The kiss ended, eventually. Most of the Cupids returned to their duties, but Fallon and Jada stayed to clean up. There was work to be done.

"Your friend will have to help us, if she's willing," Jada said. "We need her to hold the mirror. Are you even listening to me?"

"Hmm?" Fallon said. He'd been watching as Trina filled her friends in on the world they couldn't see. They sat near Susan, who still lay crying on the sidewalk.

"We have to help Susan's victims," Jada said. "And we need to get her home. She's our responsibility."

"She's her own responsibility," Fallon said. "But I agree, we should get her home."

He walked over and talked to Trina, and a few minutes later they were all walking back the way Susan had come. Cynthia and Lucy helped Susan walk; she did not look happy about it, but she had no strength to protest.

"No, no, not this way," she said. "I'm sorry, so very sorry … "

"Shut up," Fallon told her. It was mean, he knew—Susan seemed completely different now, and yelling at her was like kicking a wounded puppy. However, changed or not, Fallon wasn't ready to forgive her just yet.

It didn't take long to find the first few victims. A man sat by the sidewalk, his hands on his face. In the street, the police were dealing with the aftermath of one of the Susan-inspired car crashes.

"Let's get started," Trina said, and she crouched beside the man and touched his shoulder gently. He looked up, saw his reflection, and Jada shot some Love into him.

"You'll be all right now, sir," Trina said, noting the change on his face.

They moved on, healing those they could. Jada sensed a summons and returned to the Cupid Center, leaving Fallon to continue the healing in her place. Cynthia and Lucy went on ahead—Fallon guessed the weirdness was freaking them out. That, and they probably wanted to be rid of Susan. Her crying and apologizing were getting on everyone's nerves.

Trina and Fallon came to the first three victims: the three mean, popular girls. Three Suicides were hovering around them, feeding on their pain.

"Back off, you!" Fallon said, blasting one with his Love. It ran off and so did one of the others, but the third turned to look at them. It seemed to recognize them, and its face was eerily familiar ...

"Ricky," the Suicide said.

Fallon, who'd raised a hand to blast it, stopped. It couldn't be!

The Suicide fired a shock that struck Fallon in the chest and knocked him on his rear. When he recovered, the Suicide was gone.

"Are you all right?" Trina asked, kneeling beside him.

"No. Not exactly," Fallon replied, staring at the spot where his former boss had been.

. . .

"Jada!" Fallon called as he hurried across the Cupid Center. "Jada, where are you?"

He had to tell her what he'd seen. He was about to steal some Love to draw her attention, but then he saw her walking toward him with a young-looking Cupid girl beside her.

"Jada!" he said. "You have to know ... "

"Fallon, this is Sandra Baker," Jada said. "She was Louis's daughter."

Fallon's mouth dropped open. Sandra shuffled her feet and looked at the floor.

"She was a Suicide," Jada said. "Now she's been sent to us. Louis must have made a really good deal to get her out."

"Yeah," Fallon said, an uneasy feeling running through him. "He sure did."

30

A lot changed over the weeks that followed. Jada called upon Fallon and Owen for support in her role as leader, and worked with them to restructure the organization. Many changes were necessary to reverse the harm Louis had left as his legacy.

First and foremost, all Cupids were required to meditate for at least one hour every day. Alexander led classes to teach them how. Fallon started a class to teach Cupids to project shields.

Another big change, suggested by Fallon, involved the Love cubes. He pointed out that he would not have been able to do half the things he'd done if he hadn't stolen Love from other Cupids' cubes. Fallon suggested that the distribution of Love should be equal for all Cupids, so that newer ones like himself need never be without a steady supply. Owen said that Cupids would slack off if they always had Love available. Jada ignored him and put the plan into practice.

Jada created an office for herself so that Cupids had a place to go when they needed her. She also made a pledge, at Fallon's insistence, to look into the fates of those Cupids stuck in Limbo. Owen said that some were in there for a good reason.

"You thought I was put in there for a good reason," Fallon pointed out, and Owen fell silent.

"I'll review all the cases," Jada assured them both. "Thanks for your input. Now, get back out there and do your jobs, you two! That Love ain't gonna make itself."

"Yes, ma'am!" Owen said, tossing off a salute before turning and leaving Jada's office. Fallon followed, but Jada called him back.

"How's Sandra working out?" she asked.

"She's still a bit freaked," Fallon told her. "Post-traumatic stress, I guess. Couldn't have been easy being a Suicide. She's got promise, though. And she united her second couple yesterday."

"Good," Jada said. "Keep me posted. Now"—she held up a hand—"back to work, or else!" She snapped her fingers and a bolt of energy crackled around them.

"Yikes!" Fallon said, hopping in mock fear. "I'll get right to it!"

They laughed, then Fallon turned and left the office.

"Are we going back to the school again?" Sandra asked as she and Fallon approached the portals.

"We might," Fallon replied.

"Come on. We're going to visit your girlfriend, aren't we?"

"Yes," Fallon admitted. "But only for a few minutes. Then we'll try the corporate building a few blocks away, stir up some office romances."

"Just a few minutes, huh?" Sandra said. "I'll believe that when I see it."

Fallon smiled and said nothing. His relationship with Trina was all he could think about sometimes. And not just because he'd gotten a lot better at physical interactions, either.

But he wasn't letting that get in the way of Sandra's training. He'd asked Jada to let him be her mentor, and he took the responsibility seriously.

She hadn't taken the news about her father at all well.

"Everything he did, he did to protect you," Fallon had told her, and he believed it to be true. He hoped he didn't run into Louis when Sandra was around, though. She'd have trouble dealing with that.

Fallon and Sandra stepped through the portal into the main lobby of Guildwood Mills High School. It was full of bustling students; classes had just let out. Fallon knew he didn't have much time if he was going to visit Trina.

"I'll meet you back here," Sandra said. "You go have your fun."

"Thanks," Fallon said. "Oh, Sandra, remember..."

" … to keep my shield up and my wits about me," Sandra finished for him. "I won't forget."

Fallon knew she wouldn't. Still, the thought of her facing a Suicide left him anxious. He hoped it didn't show that much.

"Stop worrying about me!" Sandra called over her shoulder as she headed into the nearest classroom.

Fallon smiled and waved, and then he spotted the time on the wall clock. If he didn't hurry …

He waited. He was sure this was the right spot, and Trina was often the last one to …

In front of him, the door of Trina's locker opened. Trina stood there, clad only in a towel, dripping wet from the shower. Behind her, the rest of the girls' changing room was empty.

"Oh!" Trina cried, jumping in surprise. The motion knocked the towel loose and it fell to the floor. Her hands flashed across her chest as she glared at Fallon with outrage.

Fallon burst out laughing. A moment later, Trina joined him.

"I'm gonna get you for this!" she said, punching through his chest.

"You've already got me," he replied, taking her face in his hands.

"Pretty corny, Fallon," Trina said.

"Ricky," Fallon said. "Call me Ricky."

Their lips met, and Ricky Fallon had never felt so alive.

The End

About the Author

Timothy Carter was born in England during the week of the final lunar mission, and he turned thirteen on Friday the 13th. He still thinks those two things are pretty cool.

Timothy grew up in Canada's National Capital Region and studied Dramatic Arts at Algonquin College. His YA novels include *Evil?*, *Epoch*, *Attack of the Intergalactic Soul Hunters*, and *Closets*. He has also written the adult-themed novel *Section K*. Timothy lives and writes in Toronto, Canada, with his wife and two cats. To learn more about him, visit www.timothycarterworld.com.